CHANGE
PLACES
WITH
ME

BOOKS BY LOIS METZGER

Novels
A Trick of the Light
Missing Girls
Ellen's Case
Barry's Sister

Nonfiction
The Hidden Girl: A True Story of the Holocaust,
with Lola Rein Kaufman
Yours, Anne: The Life of Anne Frank

Editor
Bones: Terrifying Tales to Haunt Your Dreams
Bites: Scary Stories to Sink Your Teeth Into
Bites & Bones Flip Book
Be Careful What You Wish For: Ten Stories about Wishes
Can You Keep a Secret?: Ten Stories about Secrets
The Year We Missed My Birthday: Eleven Birthday Stories

LOIS METZGER

CHANGE
PLACES
WITH
ME

BALZER + BRAY
An Imprint of HarperCollins*Publishers*

Balzer + Bray is an imprint of HarperCollins Publishers.

Change Places with Me
Copyright © 2016 by Lois Metzger
All rights reserved. Printed in the United States of America.
No part of this book may be used or reproduced in any manner whatsoever
without written permission except in the case of brief quotations embodied
in critical articles and reviews. For information address HarperCollins
Children's Books, a division of HarperCollins Publishers, 195 Broadway,
New York, NY 10007.
www.epicreads.com

Library of Congress Control Number:2015958375
ISBN 978-0-06-238553-6

Typography by Sarah Creech
16 17 18 19 20   PC/RRDH   10 9 8 7 6 5 4 3 2 1

First Edition

To Jordan Brown

Between grief and nothing, I will take grief.
—William Faulkner

Don't worry, be happy.
—Bobby McFerrin

CONTENTS

PART 1

Forget-Me-Not

CHAPTER 1

She woke.

And for a split second saw nothing but a cloud of red light.

Where am I? She could use one of those maps with an *X*, like at the zoo, that clearly say YOU ARE HERE.

So—this is weird.

She blinked a few times, the red light dissolved, and, like a stalled hydro-bus that finally hummed to life, she caught up to herself. *I'm Rose, in my own bed—and in a granny nightgown, ugh. Gotta get rid of this thing.*

She'd slept so deeply; she took a big, slow, luxurious stretch, her long arms and legs spreading out over the bed, and brushed her pale-brown bangs away from her eyes. Yellow light poured in through the window and dust in the air sparkled—so beautiful. *It's Saturday—no, Sunday, school tomorrow. Did I finish that thing for Mr. Slocum? He'll mark me down an entire grade if something's late . . . he has it in for me, anyway; he thinks I'm not listening in class, but I am!*

Rose glanced up and saw her stepmother, Evelyn, arms crossed, leaning against the doorway in a black-and-white kimono tied tightly at her waist.

"Good morning," Rose said.

Evelyn stared as if Rose had said something shocking.

"Why are you looking at me that way?" Rose said. "You're making me feel like something we might dissect in bio."

"Well, it's just—you slept so long. It's almost two."

"You're kidding! I never do that!"

"I just wanted to be sure you're not, you know—coming down with something, or anything like that. I mean, there's always something going around. . . ."

Evelyn didn't ramble like this; she chose her words carefully and precisely. Her expression was even more serious and cautious than usual, always such a contrast to her lush auburn hair, and those blue eyes, the blue of a darkening sky. Rose had blue eyes too, but lighter.

"I'm absolutely fine, couldn't be better," Rose said. "I'm happy, really happy, practically bursting with it." She almost added, *This day feels like a gift you don't need to unwrap,* because these words had sprung into her head, but maybe that would sound too corny. Anyway, she heard something right outside, like someone saying *hoo, hoo.* "What's that sound?"

"The birds? There's a pair of mourning doves on Mrs. Moore's windowsill."

"Have they been there long?"

"Well . . . I'm pretty sure they come back every year to nest."

Rose wondered why, if that was the case, she was just noticing them now. "Morning, like the beginning of the day, or mourning as in sad?"

"Sad."

"Imagine, a whole species of birds always in mourning, never getting over it. You don't see me boo-hooing over anything, do you? Or *hoo-hoo*-ing, like the birds?" Rose smiled at her own joke, but Evelyn didn't, which almost made Rose skip a beat. "Hey, you don't have to just to stand there, you know. Don't be such a stranger, as Dad used to say." She patted her bed.

Evelyn entered slowly, hesitating, as if there was a force field in the doorway. She sat so lightly on the edge of the bed that Rose could've pushed her off with a gentle nudge.

"You smell nice," Rose said.

"Lavender. It's the soap."

"I guess I forgot." Forgot? Was that the right word? Her stomach let out a long growl. "Wow, I'm starving."

"I'm not surprised. You didn't eat much yesterday."

"Right. I was at the zoo." Rose couldn't forget that—what kid in high school went to the zoo anymore? But she had loved it. She'd seen a gorilla with a baby clinging to her neck. The baby had soft, shiny eyes, and the mother's expression said, *I will keep you safe and sound.* Rose had felt so close to the gorillas; it was like she could've taken a step and joined them. Only there must've been a glass wall or something separating them. "But you weren't with me. So how'd you know I didn't eat?"

Evelyn touched her long, slender throat; she had on a gold

necklace with a heart-shaped pendant that caught the light. "You came home so tired. You went straight to bed, no dinner."

Of course. She'd been so tired. "You don't like zoos, do you?"

"Not much."

"How come?"

"The animals might look like they're free, but they're not. That bothers me after a while."

"It might be the safest place for them."

"Yes. It's a complicated issue."

What a nice, grown-up conversation. Rose could show that she could respect another person's opinions even if she didn't agree with them. "They don't call it a zoo," she said. "They keep telling you that when you're there. It's the Bronx Global Conservation Center."

"A rose by any other name."

"What? A rose—?"

"It's an expression. It means you can change the name of something but it doesn't change what it is."

Rose shook her head. "Why should you be stuck with something that no longer fits? I wasn't born with the name Rose—but it's perfect for me."

"I'm glad," Evelyn said, but didn't sound either glad or sad.

"You get up on the wrong side of the bed or something?" Rose asked. "Dad used to say that, too. I never understood it, because I sleep next to a wall. What could I do, fall into the wall? He had some really corny expressions, like, I'll be ready in two shakes of a lamb's tail. Why would he say that? He didn't grow up on a farm—and I know I never visited one with him—we hardly ever left Belle Heights."

"He . . ." Evelyn blinked a few times. "He had a grandmother who said it."

"Really?"

"Mm-hmm. She actually did grow up on a farm. Your father adored her."

"What was her name?"

"Clara."

Rose laughed—a laugh that just burst out of her. It felt a little strange, as if someone else was laughing and she happened to be close by. But who else would it be?

Evelyn blinked again, then got up. "Would you like some eggs, Rose?"

"That would hit the spot! Something else Dad would say."

Evelyn left. Rose looked out her window at Belle Heights Tower, the building across the way that used to be five stories and then, seemingly overnight, got ten more stories added to it, and now it loomed over all the others. She'd always hated the extra floors, having grown up with the older view. An old friend of hers had moved in there and she'd never even visited her. Now Rose glanced up and noticed, for the first time, a rooftop garden bursting with leafy trees against a white sky. What a great place to be a plant, she thought. *If I were a plant, I'd want to live there.*

Rose got up and took a shower. In the soap dish, Evelyn's oval, lavender-scented soap always battled for space with her own undyed, fragrance-free soap, which sat there like a block of wax. That had been her dad's kind of unscented soap, too. Now she found herself reaching for Evelyn's. *This is what you should do,* she told herself. *Grab things, exist at the center of your life, not the edge.*

But it felt, oddly, as if someone else had told her this and she was only repeating it.

CHAPTER 2

"Mm," Rose said as she ate. "These scrambled eggs are fantastic—so rich and creamy. I love the cheddar cheese. It's like I never had them before."

"Same old, same old," Evelyn said.

"Have I told you lately you're a terrific cook?"

"No," Evelyn said, "but thank you." She was finishing up a soft-boiled egg in a special eggcup made of thin white porcelain and using a tiny silver spoon, smaller than a teaspoon, which she'd found long ago at a flea market.

Rose remembered how, as a kid, she'd thought it was gross that Evelyn got things from flea markets, but now she admired Evelyn's resourcefulness. The round kitchen table was near the window, overlooking a few trees and the sidewalk that led to Belle Heights Drive. A light breeze blew in, rustling blue curtains, and the air smelled sweet. Rose had put on overalls and a flannel shirt and found herself feeling uncomfortable, as if she had on too much fabric. She took a bite of some rye toast. "What's with these planes? That's the third one in fifteen minutes."

"There are always a lot of planes."

Which was true—Belle Heights, Queens, was between two big airports. "Is it extra noisy today?"

"Not particularly."

Rose also heard a blaring sound, like an elephant's trumpet. "What *is* that?"

"A tow truck, picking up another hydro-bus. There's a petition going around to get rid of them and bring the old buses back."

"I hope you didn't sign it. I like how they look, all red and sleek, with that ladder in the middle and the elevator for handicap accessibility."

"Those elevators never work."

"I know. But Belle Heights is never the prototype for anything, and now we're the first place in the whole city to get buses with hydrogen drives."

"I wasn't sure you liked them. When we took that one to Spruce Hills, it kept stalling—you didn't seem too pleased about that."

"Well, I should've realized—new things take time. There are always kinks to work out."

Evelyn tightened her lips as if she was about to say something but then didn't.

"It's all these steep hills in Belle Heights, that's the problem—ouch!"

"What's the matter?"

"I bit the inside of my cheek."

"You're not used to talking so much."

Evelyn didn't really need to call attention to the fact that they usually ate in silence, did she? Especially since they were having such an enjoyable, relaxed talk now. Anyway, that wasn't the problem. Rose had recently bitten this same spot before, and nothing hurt so much as biting the inside of your cheek *twice*. Except that there was also a spot on her jaw just beneath her left cheek that hurt, too; a dull, throbbing ache.

"So, Rose, I need to go to work now," Evelyn said. "Is that okay?"

"Of course," said Rose. Why wouldn't it be? "What will you be doing today?"

"I have a client interested in a condo in Spruce Hills."

"Do you like showing places to people?"

Evelyn nodded, getting up and gathering dishes.

Rose reached out, put her hand on Evelyn's arm. "I'll do that."

Evelyn looked down at Rose's hand. "You usually just wash. I clear."

"It's okay—leave it." Rose took her hand back. "So what do you like about it?"

Evelyn still gazed at the spot where Rose's hand had been. "Well . . . I like finding the right space for people."

"How do you know when the space is right?"

Now Evelyn glanced up, at the low ceiling. Their two-story apartment house had low ceilings, except the living room was sunken so it felt more spacious—and Rose realized that she appreciated Evelyn's nice way of taking a generic Queens living room and giving it a certain polish. Mounting a quilt on the wall, draping a colorful piece of silk on the cozy big blue armchair, reupholstering the couch herself with thick, flowery Italian fabric, putting down an old rug with a diamond pattern that was so big it was like wall-to-wall carpeting. She used to hate that rug and tried to avoid stepping on the diamonds, but there were too many of them. So dumb!

"All these questions, Rose," Evelyn said. "I'm not used to it."

Was she bringing this up again? "Isn't it better than not talking?"

"Yes, it's—it is better. So. I get to know the client a bit, and then try to imagine a good fit in terms of space. If clothing is said to be a second skin, a home is a third skin."

"I'm comfortable in all my skins! Did my dad ever go with you?"

"No—he worked such long hours, remember?"

"Yeah." Her dad had been a camera operator for a TV production company. "One time I said he came home at two billion a.m. He thought that was funny."

"Rose, I'm so sorry, but this client is meeting me—"

"That's okay! I'm good."

"I didn't sign it," Evelyn said.

"Sign what?"

"The petition. To get rid of the buses. Just so you know, I'm not against everything new."

Rose sat on the stoop—not a real stoop, just a few brick steps that led to the door of her redbrick apartment house in a long row of two-story apartment houses that were all connected—which, it occurred to Rose, made them truly neighbors, people who should care about one another, even if they were all squished together like houses on a Monopoly board before you traded them in for a hotel. She remembered playing that with her dad, how he always made bad trades on purpose to let her win.

Rose looked up; the October sky was the color of concrete. So the sidewalk matched the sky. Maybe it wasn't the most vivid or gorgeous color, but there was something harmonious about this, like the universe was in balance. She heard Mrs. Moore's Dobermans scuffling on the stairs behind her, and she got up. As soon as the dogs saw her, Rose knew, they would be on top of her, leashed or not.

"Oh, I didn't see you!" Mrs. Moore said. "You're never out here! Down, Cocoa! Down, Fudge!"

"They're really sweet," Rose said, though she'd almost gotten knocked down. "Which one is Cocoa? Which one is Fudge?"

"It doesn't matter. They don't listen to their names anyway."

Rose patted the dogs' strong backs, and they licked her hand. It turned out Cocoa was the one with ears that stood straight up while Fudge's drooped. She gazed into their eyes—so gentle and trusting! Some people, not Rose, might only see their size and power. Then she wondered about Mrs. Moore, who'd always lived alone. Rose wanted to reach out to her—*Because that's the kind of person I am,* she thought, as if describing herself to someone she didn't know. "Can I walk the dogs for you?"

Mrs. Moore looked at her. "I thought you were afraid of them. Just last week, you seemed so alarmed—"

"I'm not scared now, and I'd like to keep you company." Rose, at nearly six feet tall, towered over Mrs. Moore, who was tiny and stooped with a swirl of hair like white cotton candy. "I really want to try things I've never tried before." As soon as Rose said it, she knew it was true, and decided that for the next week she was going to do exactly that, every chance she got—starting today, Sunday, October 21, 2029.

"I'd be delighted," Mrs. Moore said, tilting her head up at Rose while handing over the leashes. "A word of warning—they pull."

Rose held a leash in each fist and got a good grip on them, but the dogs gave her an immediate demonstration of their strength. Basically they carried her along.

"We've never had a proper sit-down chat, have we, my dear?" Mrs. Moore said, still gazing at Rose and walking quickly to keep up. "Not that we're sitting down! But I'm so pleased. I always tried to talk to you—you never said a word."

Evelyn had brought this up, too. Why mention something from the past if it was no longer true in the present? Such a waste of time, Rose thought, as if you moved to a new house and someone kept pointing out, "You used to live over there," like you didn't know.

At dinner Rose told Evelyn about taking Mrs. Moore's dogs to Belle Heights Park. "The park looked amazing," she said. "Some leaves are turning already, burnt orange, the color of fire. I don't think the leaves have ever been this beautiful. We sat in the dog run. I got so dusty—good thing I had on overalls, though you know what? I'm getting sick of wearing them all the time. When I was walking Cocoa and Fudge, they were all over the place. I thought dogs were supposed to heel."

"When they're well trained. No doubt Mrs. Moore spoils them terribly. You weren't afraid of them?"

"I *love* animals," Rose stressed. It seemed important that Evelyn realize this and remember it. "Did you sell that place today?"

"Yes."

"That's great! You found the right space for that person. This pasta—it's amazing. What is it, just garlic and oil?"

"And a little red pepper, to give it a kick."

Evelyn still had on work clothes—a crisp white blouse, black pants, gray blazer, flats. That gorgeous hair spilled over her shoulders, and that smell of lavender, so exquisite. Rose noticed, too, lines around Evelyn's mouth and eyes. When had Evelyn gotten older? Her skin had always been smooth as a lake. "You know, I saw a video the other day. There's this new thing. You go into a special room and high-pitched sounds zap your skin, get rid of your wrinkles. Not that you're all wrinkly or anything."

Evelyn touched her face lightly. "I don't mind wrinkles. Besides, people complain of hearing loss, after."

"They didn't say anything about side effects."

"They never do, do they? Some of these new procedures—I don't trust them—they pop up out of nowhere and you're supposed to just put your life in their hands. . . ."

"Whoa," Rose said. "Did I touch a nerve?"

"Sorry, that just came out," Evelyn said. "Never mind."

"Well, on a far more important subject, it's time to cut my hair."

"Cut it yourself, you mean?"

That was what she always did, a pair of scissors and a ruler for the bangs, which fell into her eyes, and occasionally she grabbed the ends, too, and took off an inch or so. "No, I want a real haircut this time, at Sassy Cuts. No bangs, but long enough so I could put it behind my ears if I want, or have it behind one ear and not the other."

"That's certainly specific. Let me give you some money." Evelyn pulled her wallet out of her bag and gave Rose a few folded bills.

"I'll pay you back. I'm thinking I could get a job."

"Oh?"

"Not sure what yet." Inside the bills was a small folded piece of yellow paper. Rose opened it. A receipt from a place called Forget-Me-Not, for $1,600. That spot on her jaw began to ache again, and she winced.

"Your cheek still hurts," Evelyn said, concerned.

"It's okay. What is this?" She held the paper up.

Evelyn glanced up quickly. "Oh, was something in there?"

"It says Forget-Me-Not."

"It's nothing."

"You spent sixteen hundred dollars there. Yesterday. When I was at the zoo. The gorillas were so close, it was like I could touch them."

"It's a flower shop." Evelyn took hold of the receipt.

"That's a lot of money to spend at a flower shop."

"I keep an account there. I send housewarming gifts to clients. It adds up."

"Can I see it again?"

But Evelyn had already put it back in her wallet and snapped her bag shut.

CHAPTER 3

Belle Heights High School was enormous, bursting at the seams with over two thousand students, but on Monday morning Rose found something wonderfully energizing about all these personalities in one place. Overcrowding or not, there was something new to notice anywhere you looked—a girl with silver jewelry in her braids, a guy with a forehead tattoo that said *If you can read this, you're too close.* Rose hoped it was a Sün-Fade tattoo; some things just weren't meant to be permanent. She sighed, feeling so good—never mind that that strange red light had been there again that morning, behind her eyes and still there once she opened them. How could it be both inside and outside? But all she'd had to do was blink a few times and it was gone.

Morning classes went by in a flash, instead of dragging endlessly, and she talked to kids as if she fit right in, just like they did: "Tough math test!" "Did you finish that bio thing?"

At lunch in the cafeteria, the student who worked the scanner looked at her, down at her tray, and back at her again. He had dark bushy hair and eyebrows so thick they almost formed a unibrow, and he was several inches shorter than Rose.

"Never thought you were the scuffin type," he said. "A scone or a muffin, maybe, but not the combo."

"It looked good," Rose said.

"Garbo talks!"

"Garbo?"

"Greta Garbo—a silent movie star. Silent, like you—before now, that is. When she finally made a talkie, everybody got so excited to hear her voice, the posters said, 'Garbo Talks!'" He picked up the scuffin and tossed it around like a baseball. "This thing is dry as dust. You'll need this." He put a pineapple juice stick on her tray. He was talking like they knew each other. They didn't, really, but Rose smiled at him. "She smiles! Stop the presses!" He was starting to sound like someone in an old movie himself. "Except, let's try a second take."

"What?"

"That smile looks, well . . . kind of Photoshopped or something. Hey, sorry." He put his hands up like he was surrendering.

The line bunched up behind Rose, and she moved on.

She noticed Kim Garcia at the end of a long table, which was where she always sat, and gave her a big wave and an even bigger smile. But Rose wasn't able to catch her friend's eye. She made her way over through the crowds and sat on the bench opposite Kim, her long legs bunched up beneath the table.

"How was your weekend?" Rose asked.

Kim had a long, ropy braid down her back, pale-gray eyes, and light-brown skin, and she always wore colors that didn't quite match—olive green and red, for instance. But Rose thought she looked really good.

As usual, Kim brought her own lunch; today she had a tuna sandwich and blueberry yogurt. "My weekend?" she said.

Rose took a bite of the scuffin. It crumbled to gravelly bits in her mouth, and she had to work hard to swallow it. Still, it was sweet, and the juice stick that turned from solid to liquid helped, she had to admit. "Did you have fun? I went to the zoo. It was really great. I never get tired of seeing the gorillas."

Kim blinked at her. "I wasn't sure you were speaking to me."

"Of course I am! You're my oldest friend."

"You got so freaked out at my place, and then you just left, no explanation—"

"Don't worry about it. It's long over."

"It was only last Friday."

"Feels like a lifetime ago. Speaking of which, I'd like to be called Rose from now on."

"Rose? Why?"

"It suits me, like a second skin."

Kim sighed. "How many skins do you need?"

"Hey, remember when we were in second grade, and we had to do that post office project, and we were supposed to write letters to kids in first grade, but we got in trouble because we only wrote letters to each other, so then Ms. Zimmer separated us and I threw a fit? My dad said I needed extra care and attention because I was 'sensitive,' but I don't think Ms. Zimmer agreed with him." Rose took another bite of the juice stick. "You remember my dad, don't you?"

"Rose . . ." Kim shook her head, as if brushing dust out of her hair, and took a deep breath. "Yes. Of course I remember him. He called me Kimmy—nobody else did." She took what was left of Rose's juice stick. "He always had these great little jokes. Like, a man wants to take piano lessons. He's told the first lesson costs fifty dollars but the second lesson is only five. He says, 'Can't we start with the second lesson?'" Kim started to smile, but it didn't turn into an actual smile. "I remember you, too."

"Well, I should hope so!" Rose looked across the cafeteria. "That wall video for the boys' basketball team. Isn't that Nick Winter? The cute one?"

Nick Winter was one of the most popular guys in tenth grade. He was in Rose's bio class and virtual lab, last period of the day. His hair was always messy in what looked like a carefully planned way, and he was tall, like Rose, with a diamond in his front tooth. She'd seen it once, sparkling in sunlight. He was gorgeous. What would that diamond look like up close, if he leaned in to kiss her?

"I wonder if I should try out for the girls' basketball team," Rose said, thinking it would give her something in common with Nick.

"Basketball? You?"

"Why not? I'm tall. In middle school the coaches were all

over me to join the team."

"The tryouts were in September. It's way too late."

"Oh, too bad. Well, there's always next year." Rose smiled—a smile she was sure did *not* look Photoshopped.

"I'll try to remember," Kim said, half to herself.

"Remember what?"

"To call you Rose."

In bio, Rose's lab partners were Selena Kearn and Astrid Mills, who were best friends and the two most popular girls in tenth grade. Selena, an ex-girlfriend of Nick's, was all bouncy red curls and freckles; Astrid was a blond beauty with stick-straight hair and glowing skin. She always wore black; today, a black dirndl with black leather ties. Astrid was sure not to question Rose's name change, as Kim had, because once upon a time Astrid had been Abigail; she'd changed her name in sixth grade. She'd understand.

Rose found herself staring at Nick Winter at the next virtual lab table, willing him to look at her. But why should he notice her now, any more than he ever had? She didn't look any different, in the same overalls and the same flannel shirt and the same bangs she had to push out of her eyes—why'd she always let them get so long?

"Is she seriously serious?" Selena said to Astrid. "Nick?"

Rose gave her head a little tilt. "He's not too hideous."

"Oh my God," Selena said. "Now she thinks she can just chime in."

"She must be ill," Astrid murmured. She often spoke in a low voice; people had to lean in to hear her.

"Never felt better!" Rose said brightly, and turned to Selena. "How come you broke up with Nick?"

Astrid let out a sharp laugh. "Who told you that?"

Selena's face burned behind her freckles. "It was a mutual decision. We decided it would be best if we saw other people."

"Sure," Astrid said, "except he started seeing other people before arriving at this so-called mutual decision."

"Why are we even having this conversation with *her*?" Selena asked. "She's not part of anything!"

Just then the bio teacher, Mr. Slocum, was standing before them. Rose could swear she saw her own reflection in his shiny, bald head. "I trust you're discussing your observations on the dissection? The outline is due in fifteen minutes."

"No problem!" Selena said. "Such an interesting project!"

Mr. Slocum took a moment to give Rose a hard look. "You've been paying attention, I hope?"

"Absolutely," Rose said.

"You think I can't tell when my students are off in la-la land? I've been teaching for thirty years."

"That's wonderful!" Selena said. "You're so dedicated." As soon as he left, she said, "What observations? The whole project was a disaster!"

"You should write the outline," Astrid said to Rose. "You were the one who messed it up last week."

True, last week's assignment had not gone well. "Okay, just

catch me up on what I missed," Rose said. "By the way, you may find this interesting, Astrid, since you changed your name a few years back. My new name is Rose. It suits me like a—"

"Whatever," Astrid muttered.

That was easy, Rose thought, relieved.

CHAPTER 4

Everyone said Belle Heights was so boring, a big chunk of nothing in Queens, New York City. Belle Drive, the busiest street, was a museum, a fossil, a dinosaur compared to neighboring Spruce Hills, which had giant stores like Target, Home Depot, and Asteroid, and smaller, trendy stores opening all the time. But Rose decided she liked the fact that, except for the hydrobuses (and she could hear one wheezing behind her, a sure sign it was about to stall), long, winding Belle Drive had changed so little over the years. Especially now that she was changing so much. She'd spoken to a lady recently somewhere who seemed to know about these things—that Rose would change, that she would be so happy. If Rose ran into the lady again, she could tell her she was right. But how could you run into someone if you didn't remember what she looked like?

No matter. It rained so lightly Rose didn't even get wet as she passed a diner with a revolving display of layer cakes, a thrift shop, a cosmetics store, and an animal hospital—little places so close together they all seemed connected, like the apartment houses on Rose's block. Some even shared an awning.

Inside Sassy Cuts, Rose spoke to a hairstylist whose nametag said *Bridget*.

"That was my mother's name!" Rose said, amazed at the coincidence. Rose had no memory of her mother, who'd died when she was a baby, but there were pictures, of course, and apparently her mom had laughed a lot.

"What can I do for you?" Bridget said.

"I need to get rid of these bangs." Rose flicked them away as if that was all it took to rid her life of them.

"Not a problem. They're awfully long, anyway. You can hardly see your nice blue eyes!"

Rose described the exact, even, almost chin length she wanted, "So I can put my hair behind one ear if I want to. Please don't go too short or I won't be able to do that."

"I'll be careful."

"It should be dark. Can you dye it, too?"

"Of course."

As Rose sat in the chair, an oldies station blasted away. She'd never paid much attention to music, but now she could barely sit still from an urge to nod her head and shimmy-shake. One song in particular really stuck with her, even though it was almost sixty years old. "Changes" by David Bowie. *"Strange fascination, fascinating me . . . pretty soon now you're gonna get older . . . ch-ch-ch-ch-changes . . ."* She couldn't wait to download it to her phone.

Bridget gave her a quick blow-dry and said, "What do you think?"

In the mirror Rose saw a girl with short dark hair just above her chin. She pushed one side behind her ear and left the other side in front. "It's perfect."

She also stopped in at the thrift store just down the street, Second Nature. She had to have a jean jacket. But not just any old jean jacket. It had to suit the new haircut, complement it. She tried on half a dozen jean jackets, and every time she looked in the mirror and turned around to see her back, something was missing. Very disappointing, but she would keep looking for exactly the right one.

On Tuesday morning Rose had to sign up for six hours of school service, which was a tenth-grade requirement this semester. A great opportunity, she thought, to try something new and exciting. She read the list of choices: caring for soil-free plants in the school greenhouse, after-school tutoring, assistant crossing guard. But something else grabbed her. Mr. Slocum needed a lab assistant. No students ever signed up to work with him—why would they? Mr. Slocum was the most hated teacher in school, and he seemed to have a particular dislike for her. Maybe by the end of the six hours, Mr. Slocum would tolerate her better, even like her. Which was as worthy a project as any.

Rose sat down to lunch with Kim again. Kim, true to form, was wearing a purple shirt over maroon pants and, around her throat, a blue scarf with black stars. Rose knew she herself had to stop wearing overalls and flannel shirts, but Kim's style was not the direction she had in mind.

"Do you like my hair?" Rose asked. "The guy at the scanner said I look like Barbara Stanwyck, whoever that is."

"You mean Cooper Sosa?"

"Who?"

"At the scanner. He's cute."

Rose glanced at him and shrugged. His eyebrows were way too thick and his hair too messy (and not in a good way, like Nick's). Not to mention she'd be surprised if he reached her chin.

"Maybe not conventionally cute," Kim said. "He only transferred here last year. We hang out sometimes. He's super nice."

"Really? Yesterday he said my smile looked Photoshopped." Rose hadn't thought that had bothered her, but here she was, repeating it.

"And today he said you look like a movie star. He's really into old movies. His parents own a diner right next to the old movie house—"

"You still haven't said." Rose pointed to her hair.

"Oh, yeah. It's fine."

"I tried to find a jean jacket yesterday, and I couldn't. Don't you think a jean jacket would look great with this haircut? Also, I need red lipstick. Something between a cherry and a tomato. But not cherry tomato—ugh!"

"You don't wear makeup," Kim said, suddenly agitated. "You just don't. Even when you barely spoke to me, I noticed you don't wear it, and I always liked that, because we're, like, the only girls who don't."

Rose was fully aware that she and Kim hadn't been that close recently. Why did she have to bring it up? "Ironic," she said coolly, "seeing that you're doing the makeup for the school play. You're like a makeup expert, Kim."

"Stage makeup is a whole other thing. It's not realistic and it's not supposed to be—"

"Do you think Nick Winter will like my hair?" Rose cut her off.

Nick still didn't notice her in bio. Astrid and Selena didn't say a word about her hair, though they were whispering. Rose didn't want to intrude; maybe one had a problem and the other was helping her. That was what friends did for each other, after all. How lonely it must be, Rose thought, to be without friends.

On her way home, Rose stopped in at the cosmetics store on Belle Drive: Heights Belles. She wandered through a sea of red lipsticks before she found the right one—exciting, rich, deep red. When she saw the name, she had to laugh. It was called Rose Red; clearly, meant for her. She stood before the Mirror-Mirror and typed in the code of the lipstick, and it showed her how perfectly this shade fit her haircut. But something about seeing herself on a computer screen bothered Rose. In her mind she saw herself on another screen, but wider than this one. She figured maybe she'd accidentally stepped in front of a security camera and seen a reflection of herself, which could be a little disconcerting when you didn't expect it.

Outside, she got caught in a gentle tornado of fallen leaves; they swirled lightly around her legs and settled at her feet. *You are at the center of your life, not the edge,* she told herself, but the words seemed to be coming from the same lady she remembered speaking to somewhere—someone with a sort of funny, flat, generic voice.

Rose found herself staring at the Belle Heights Animal Hospital two doors down, in the basement of a building, with windows near the ceiling and apartments up above. She'd told Evelyn she was thinking about getting a job; what a great idea, to work there! After all, she loved animals. Now *this* was a perfect project, too.

She stopped in and met Stacey, the very pretty twenty-something receptionist, with cropped reddish-brown hair and large brown eyes, and the owner, Dr. Lola, who was tall, though not as tall as Rose, and had dark-blond hair tied back in a scarf that couldn't hold it all.

"Your timing is uncanny! Somebody just quit," Dr. Lola said. "Do you have any experience working with animals?"

"Not a whole lot." Other than taking a couple of Dobermans to the dog run in Belle Heights Park two days ago.

"Why do you want to work here?"

Rose had to think. After a moment she said, "I don't think people can be happy unless their animals are happy."

Dr. Lola grinned. "That's the best answer I ever heard. How old are you? You'll have to get working papers if you're under sixteen."

"I'm fifteen."

"I can give you temporary papers right away. I can't pay much. The hours would be Saturday all day and one weekday afternoon, as needed. Can you manage that?"

Rose had to work with Mr. Slocum this week, so she said, "Starting this Saturday."

"Rouge, come meet Rose! Rose is going to work here."

Rouge turned out to be a Doberman, too. Rouge meant red—first the lipstick, now the dog, as if the pieces of Rose's life were magically connected.

Dr. Lola explained that Rouge lived there and gave blood when animals needed transfusions. The brown patches in her coat were a beautiful tawny color.

Rose scratched Rouge under the chin, and the dog leaned her sleek, muscular body against Rose. *See? I love animals,* she thought, as if someone had walked in on this cozy scene and claimed otherwise.

CHAPTER 5

Rose spent Tuesday evening rummaging through Evelyn's closet. Evelyn didn't have a ton of clothes but more of a simple, careful selection, only a few new items but mostly things that had been well cared for over the years. There were basics, like pressed black pants and tailored blouses, and lots of colors, nothing too loud or gaudy, soft purples and browns and blues and pale reds, and a bunch of different textures, mohair sweaters, corduroy shirts, silky skirts, knit shawls that draped Rose's shoulders, a velvet jacket that felt wonderfully soft, and tweed wool blazers that fit Evelyn at the hips and hit Rose at the waist. She tried on nearly everything (except the kimonos, which Evelyn wore at home, relaxing), even the low-heeled, plain leather shoes with straps at the ankles, which didn't fit, but there were some old cowboy boots Rose slid right on. Amazing, how good these clothes looked on her, considering that Rose was a few inches taller than Evelyn.

Too bad Evelyn didn't have that perfect jean jacket.

"I always wanted to share my things with you," Evelyn said, adjusting the waistband of a silky navy-blue skirt on Rose. "I had a feeling you would look great in them."

"I guess I got stuck on those old, drab clothes for a while," Rose said.

"I tried to get you to come shopping in Spruce Hills—"

"I was stubborn, wasn't I?" Rose laughed, that strange laugh that felt like someone else's.

"That you were," Evelyn said.

Before first period the next day, Rose walked over to Astrid and Selena, enjoying the lively swish of a silky skirt, and a light-gray blouse, and cowboy boots. A second skin that fit like the first one. It made her feel better; she'd had a bad moment that morning. The red light had lasted longer instead of immediately fading. But now it felt as if it had never existed.

"I'm seriously dying to go to a Halloween party," Selena was saying. "I've got my costume and everything—a leather jump-suit and love beads, like the girl singer in the Cadaver Dogs."

"You're not gonna wear anything if you don't have anywhere to go," Astrid said gloomily.

Selena glanced at Rose. "What do you want?"

"Just saying hi," Rose said, and got a great idea. "I heard you guys talking about Halloween. Why don't you come to a party at my house? You know, you and a bunch of other kids."

Astrid raised an eyebrow.

"I could have a party," Rose repeated. "I mean, if you can't have a party at your own houses—"

"There is that," Selena burst out. "My mother's so worried about her precious furniture! She says she doesn't want a bunch of kids running around breaking things."

"As if we were still two years old." Astrid sighed.

"Why doesn't she get House-in-a-Can?" Rose suggested. "The inflatable furniture would be great for a party."

"My cousin bought it after seeing a video," Selena said. "The couch exploded. They were cleaning up pieces weeks after."

"You don't have to tell her your whole life story," Astrid said.

"And *your* mom's too cheap to throw a party," Selena said, "even with all that alimony. I don't know how she gets to collect from more than one ex-husband! She must have some insane lawyer!"

"You don't know when to shut up, do you?" Astrid said.

"So," Rose said cheerfully, making light of the moment, "what about Saturday night at my place?"

Astrid and Selena exchanged a look.

"Where do you live?" Astrid said.

"How big is it?" Selena said.

Rose described her living room and how she lived across from Belle Heights Tower.

"Hey," Selena said, taking a step closer to Rose and touching her hair, "I like those boots—they look ancient. And your hair's really cute."

"Thanks! I just had it done." Rose also explained about the clothes.

"My mother's stuff is hideous," Selena said. "It would be like wearing a granny nightgown in public."

Rose didn't mention that just a few nights ago she'd slept in a granny nightgown. Since then she'd switched to a big T-shirt.

"This party could actually be fun!" Selena said.

Nick Winter came by to talk to Selena. "Did you give Dylan that picture of me with bedhead?"

Selena smiled shyly. "Maybe I did, maybe I didn't."

"That idiot posted it." Nick looked over at Rose curiously, as if he knew something was different but couldn't place it. "You're that girl, right?"

"Which girl is that?" Rose replied, trying not to get distracted by the diamond in his tooth and everything else about Nick Winter that was so gorgeous.

"You always looked like a farmer girl."

Amazing, all these years in the same schools and he didn't even know her name. Well, he could start with her new one. "Rose Hartel," she told him.

As he turned to leave, he said, "You don't look like a farmer girl anymore, Rose Hartel."

Promising.

"Why don't you sign out and have lunch with us?" Selena said to Rose. "We can plan this party."

Rose tried to get Kim to come out, too.

"With Selena and Astrid? Are you kidding?" Kim said. Today she had on a tie-dyed parachute dress. It looked homemade.

"Why, what's wrong with them?"

"Um, let's see, how about everything?"

"Astrid and Selena are the most popular girls in tenth grade, and everybody wants to hang out with them. Does that mean there's something wrong with everybody?"

"Yeah, there is."

"Well, then I'm happy to have something wrong with me, too!" Actually she felt honored. Lots of kids hung around Selena and Astrid, but today Rose had actually been asked to lunch. "I'll let you know where we are. You can meet us if you change your mind."

Kim looked hard at Rose. "I'll be here—maybe checking out today's crossword puzzle. I'm a natural, remember?"

"Of course. I remember everything. Why wouldn't I?" The week before, she and Kim had done a puzzle together. Although before that, she'd always done them by herself, off at a corner table that faced a brick wall.

They ate in a Thai restaurant. It was dimly lit with gleaming cherrywood tables and a heavenly smell of coconut and ginger; Rose basked in the scent. She didn't recognize anything on the menu. "What should I get?"

"You want us to *order* for you?" Selena asked.

"Maybe she hasn't had this kind of food before." Astrid cast a glance at Selena. "She's being adventurous."

Rose liked the sound of that. Adventurous.

"Speaking of ordering stuff," Selena said, "for the party, you've gotta get cupcakes from Fully Baked." It was the best bakery in Belle Heights, according to Selena.

"Says the girl who shouldn't eat cupcakes," Astrid said.

"You always make me feel like such a blimp!" Selena said.

"But you're not fat," Rose said.

"Next to *her* I am."

"No need to compare yourself like that," Rose said. "What you see in the looking glass isn't important—it's who you are that matters."

"Looking glass?" Astrid said, stifling a laugh.

"I mean mirror." Where had that come from? Rose could almost hear someone else saying it. But who would use such an old-fashioned word?

"Getting back to the party," Astrid said, "you have to get some entertainment."

Selena wanted a DJ; when Rose said that might cost too much, Selena said, "I know! You can have a psychic! My cousin went to a party and said the psychic was incredible. One look and she could recite your whole past."

Rose had no need for her past. But her future—why not?

The food arrived. Rose ate slowly and savored the garlic, basil, and peanut sauces. Amazing how many things there were to experience if you were adventurous. Selena said it was good she had Skipping that afternoon.

"It's the best exercise!" she said. "They play music seriously loud and you skip around the room."

"You need somebody to teach you how to skip?" Astrid said.

"It's a special way to skip! You'd know if you tried it."

Rose thought it was good they felt comfortable enough to tease each other in front of her.

"You can come skip with me," Selena said to Rose.

"It's tempting," Rose said, imagining herself skipping to "Changes." She'd been listening to it on her phone whenever she had a chance, even disabling the ads so she could play it on a loop. "But I've got school service."

"There are ways to get out of that," Astrid said. "I haven't done it since fifth grade."

"No, it's okay." Rose was looking forward to it, actually. She was going to uncover the humanity in Mr. Slocum. *Because that's the kind of person I am.*

When it came time to pay, Astrid was short, and Selena just had a credit card. The place was cash only.

"We'll treat tomorrow," Selena said.

CHAPTER 6

Were Rose's taste buds working overtime? Every meal was a feast, even the quick dinner of spinach-and-cheese ravioli Evelyn had made that night. "Mm, this is incredible," Rose said. "Hey, let's have a party this weekend."

"What?" Evelyn looked tired, shadows under her dark-blue eyes. Hadn't she been sleeping well? Rose slept like a rock as soon as her bedside lamp was off.

"For Halloween. With music—and a psychic. My friend Selena knows someone really good. Is that okay with you?"

"Um, sure." Though it sounded like Evelyn had been about to ask her something but then had stopped herself.

"I had a really great day," Rose said, as if that was what Evelyn had been thinking about. "Not even Mr. Slocum could ruin it. I helped him organize papers, and he barely spoke to me. What a stick-in-the-mud, as Dad used to say. Something else that came from his grandma Clara, I guess."

"Mr. Slocum is the one who sent you down to Ms. Pratt's office."

Ms. Pratt—the school psychologist. Rose was supposed to check in with Ms. Pratt this Friday. "Mr. Slocum thinks I don't listen in class. I tried to tell him that I do listen, but he cut me right off."

"Maybe it's best to let him be. He'll speak to you when he's ready."

"But I want him to talk to me *now*."

"Why?"

Because, Rose told herself firmly, *Mr. Slocum is alone, and I can help.* But she didn't say this out loud. Instead she said, "That reminds me. I should go upstairs and check with Mrs. Moore, see if she'd mind a loud party down here."

"But her dogs—"

"I love animals! I'm starting work at a vet's office!"

"I know. If you get scared, you can always call me."

Rose shook her head. Had Evelyn always been such a worrier?

Upstairs, Rose knocked on Mrs. Moore's door and heard the dogs scuffling behind it. When the door opened, she was as happy to see them as they were to jump on her. They seemed to remember that she'd taken them to the dog run—or rather, that they'd pulled her there.

"Oh, my dear, come in!" Mrs. Moore said. Rose realized she'd never seen Mrs. Moore indoors and close up like this. Her skin looked thin, papery. She wore a flowery housedress that zipped up the front, and she smelled like minty toothpaste. "How lovely to see you. Is that a new hairdo?"

"You like it?"

"You have such lovely blue eyes. I never knew."

"Mrs. Moore, I'd like to have a party this Saturday night. It might get loud. If that's a problem, I'll cancel it." Rose really hoped she wouldn't have to.

"The benefits of old age—you get quite deaf," said Mrs. Moore. "The noise won't bother me at all. Would you like to come in and sit down?"

"I'd love to."

Rose followed Mrs. Moore to the living room. The place had the same layout as Rose's, but the unfamiliar furniture made it look entirely different. Mrs. Moore had wooden benches with cushions and tiny Persian rugs. Here the rugs were out of place, scattered to the corners, no doubt because of the dogs—who had gone to another room. "Probably to sit on my bed, where they're not allowed," Mrs. Moore said. "How nice, my dear, having you here."

Rose was thinking the same thing. How important it was to be a good listener. For a moment she got lost in this thought, and when she tuned in again, she heard, "—you poor thing, so much sadness in your young life."

"We all have sadness," Rose said lightly. "But you can't let it destroy you; you have to let it go. Grief is a balloon just waiting to be popped."

"Oh? I can't say I know what that means. I lost my husband,

41

too, so long ago. He was an artist. He did the painting behind you, of Belle Heights Bay."

Rose swiveled around to see a swirly picture. Was that a sailboat? Was that lots of water? She couldn't make it out. People used to swim in Belle Heights Bay, but it hadn't been clean enough for that in decades. As a kid, she'd heard that if you put your feet in the water, your toenails would dissolve. Her dad always said that was an urban myth, that he'd gone swimming there—"And at last count, I had ten toenails! Though they all turned green." She'd shrieked and insisted he show her he was only kidding. Unfortunately for her dad, she asked to see them again and again.

"That painting is really pretty," Rose said.

"Some people find his work blurry. I have to admit, I'm one of them!"

Rose didn't say she was one of them, too.

Mrs. Moore launched into several stories, including something about going to an eye doctor, to check on that blurriness. Rose's attention wandered again. She thought about what she might wear to the Halloween party. She hadn't gotten dressed up since she was a little kid, a ghost in an old sheet with holes cut out. "A classic costume that couldn't be improved upon," her dad had said, when she'd wanted to go to Party-A-Rama and buy something. Maybe she should go as a farmer—an inside joke with Nick? Rose was pulled back into the conversation when she heard Mrs. Moore say, "It's a funny thing about memories. Why do we remember certain things and forget so much else?"

"Memory is a dog," Rose said.

"What, dear?"

"Memory brings us things we don't want and plops them in front of us, wagging its tail."

"The things you say! Grief is a balloon. Memory is a dog."

"Anyway," Rose said, "thanks for being so understanding about Saturday night, and for telling me that story about your husband."

"My niece, you mean."

"Yeah, of course."

"I have other paintings—in the hall, in the bedroom. Would you like to see them?"

Poor Mrs. Moore was positively starved for company. This was what happened when you gave people a little taste of something they craved—they wanted more and more and more. In a small corner of her mind, she knew exactly what that felt like, to want something so desperately and have no idea how to get it—

"Toothache?" Mrs. Moore said.

"What?" Rose, unaware, had been rubbing her jaw.

"See a dentist, my dear. Make sure it's not the roots."

Rose stood. "About those paintings? One or two would be nice." She didn't want this visit to last forever, after all.

CHAPTER 7

Rose went out for lunch with Selena and Astrid again on Thursday—who knew there was a Korean place in Belle Heights, tucked between a gas station and a parking lot near the expressway?

"I've been meaning to ask you," Astrid said. "What's with that ID pic on your phone?"

True, it wasn't flattering. She'd had it taken at Kim's apartment when they were experimenting with some stage makeup.

"Yeah," Selena said. "It's seriously disgusting."

"I almost threw up when you called me and that thing came up," Astrid said. "Delete it now."

"I will. After we eat." Rose didn't want to interrupt things, not when she was ordering *sukuh chi gae*—seafood with vegetables in spicy broth. In Korean it sounded so sophisticated! Add that to adventurous.

"This party is gonna be so much fun," Selena said. "I sent out the insta-vites, and tons of kids are coming."

"Did you invite Kim Garcia?" Rose asked.

"Her? You know that her father drives a tow truck," Astrid said. "He shows up whenever a hydro-bus breaks down."

"And the stuff she wears . . ." Selena left it at that.

It hadn't occurred to Rose that Selena and Astrid wouldn't start warming up to Kim. But Rose could do something about that, help bring them together; this party was a good first step. "I want Kim to come," she said.

"Fine," Selena said under her breath.

The food arrived. Rose wrapped her long fingers around the chopsticks, got the hang of them after a while, and imagined the three of them coming back here with Kim, and they'd do other stuff outside of school too, go to a movie, listen to music, or just hang out—a new group of best friends.

Selena and Astrid forgot to treat Rose but at least paid for themselves. Mostly.

After school it was time to get Mr. Slocum to talk to her. Rose had a friendly conversation planned in her head. "Mr. Slocum—" she began.

"Not now." He spoke from behind his wraparound computer screen.

"When?"

He pointed to a pile of work on one of the student desks. Rose had to grade a surprise quiz from a morning class and do some filing.

Patiently, Rose waited. She graded the quizzes. She filed. Two hours went by and still Mr. Slocum said nothing. But why? Mrs. Moore had loved the attention, couldn't get enough of it.

"I guess I'll see you tomorrow," Rose said at the end of the afternoon, trying not to sound disappointed.

"That's the arrangement."

He never even looked at her.

On the way home, she brightened when she caught sight of a dog in a sweater. "It's so great you put a sweater on him!" she told the owner, a guy on his phone, who didn't really want to be interrupted. "That means you're taking good care of him."

During one of her free periods on Friday, Rose had to check in with Ms. Pratt, the school psychologist.

"Goodness," Ms. Pratt said. "You look well."

"I feel well." Rose knew this office—the pale-blue walls; the indentation in the couch; the tall flowers, now a bit brown around the edges, held in a glass vase filled with water and stones; and Ms. Pratt herself, dark wavy hair, olive skin, always wearing muted colors like beige and taupe. It had never occurred to Rose before, but now she wondered if Ms. Pratt's understated style was her way of saying *The important thing in this room is* you.

"You were here while I was away," Ms. Pratt said. "You spoke with Ms. Gruskin; I read her notes. You had a disagreement with Mr. Slocum?"

"I'm working on that. I'm doing my school service with him."

"Really?" Ms. Pratt couldn't hide her surprise. "Tell me

what's been happening with you."

"Well, I'm Rose now."

"Rose?"

"Don't you think it suits me?"

"I think it's a wonderful name for you. I see you've changed your hair, your clothes—"

"You look different too." Rose realized that Ms. Pratt had a kind of glow about her.

Ms. Pratt couldn't hide a small smile. "Is it that obvious? Well, it's not exactly a secret, why I was away. My wife and I went to a reservation in Arizona to adopt a baby."

"That's fantastic! Tell me about the baby."

"We're not here to talk about that."

"Can I see a picture?"

"We only have a few minutes—"

Rose clasped Ms. Pratt's hands. "Please?"

"Oh, all right." Ms. Pratt had several pictures on her phone, actually. "That's my wife, holding Ethan—she took an extended leave to take care of him."

"She's keeping him safe and sound." Rose gazed at Ms. Pratt's beautiful son.

"Now let's get back to you and Mr. Slocum," Ms. Pratt said.

"Today's my last day of school service, and Mr. Slocum and I are going to have a nice, long talk. We'll be peachy after that."

"Peachy, huh?"

"My dad used to say that. Ask him, how are you, he'd say, peachy. I'd get mad and tell him, you can't feel like a piece of fruit! Anyway, why a peach? Why not an apple, or a tangerine?"

"I have a feeling you weren't the easiest child."

"Maybe so. But my dad never complained." Rose leaned forward eagerly. "Ethan—what a great name. So what was he like on the plane ride home? Does he sleep through the night? I'd love to see him in person. Will you bring him to school?" Rose had more questions after that, and then the free period was over.

At the end of her final day of school service, Rose plunged right in. Last chance! "Mr. Slocum, why don't you tell me about yourself?"

He glanced up from behind his computer. "Whatever for?"

"You think I don't listen—"

"I don't think it, Miss Hartel. I know it. Lately there's been improvement, I'll admit. But for all of September and most of October, you were off in la-la land."

"Not true. I'm sorry it looked that way."

"I had to send you to Ms. Pratt. Nothing personal," he added.

Nothing personal? He'd singled her out in front of the whole class for a trip to the school psychologist. "I'm here now—you can talk to me."

"Why should I want to talk to you now?"

Mr. Slocum wasn't making this easy. "Well, you're a science teacher. Maybe you could tell me about . . . Mount Vesuvius." She wasn't sure why she'd said that; she'd never thought much about volcanoes, but for some reason it was there in her mind.

Mr. Slocum glared at her; his big, round, shiny head turned

purple. "I wasn't an eyewitness to the destruction of Pompeii, if that's what you're implying."

"Of course not!"

"Miss Hartel, you need six hours of school service. That's the tenth-grade requirement, unless I'm such an old ruin I'm remembering it wrong."

Rose was afraid she might trigger another eruption here in the lab, but she pushed on. "Maybe you can tell me where you were born, why you became a teacher, that kind of thing?"

He looked at her intently. "You're quite full of yourself."

"Not true! I'm modest!"

"Don't sound so proud of it."

Maybe Rose should leave it alone, as Evelyn had suggested. Clearly Mr. Slocum wanted nothing to do with her. Still, it was important to try to get through, reach out to the humanity within. The best thing was probably to be direct. "You must be very lonely," she said.

But Mr. Slocum looked at her as if she was the one to be pitied.

That night Rose and Evelyn went to work transforming the apartment. Selena had suggested battery-operated dancing skeletons and glow-in-the-dark pumpkins from Party-A-Rama. Rose had thought they could go shopping together, but Selena said, "Sorry, no time!"

Evelyn was hanging a disco ball from the ceiling light. At lunch Astrid had said disco balls add atmosphere; they'd gone to a Caribbean place. Rose made a point of telling them that next time they really had to bring more cash.

"Did you call the psychic?" Rose asked.

"I did," Evelyn replied.

"I want to pay for her. Now that I have a job, I think that's only right." Evelyn really ought to get some sleep, Rose thought. Those bags under her eyes—she looked almost bruised. Evelyn was still relatively young and undeniably beautiful, and to look older and beaten up was just wrong. "The music—I wonder what kids listen to these days. Wow, I sound a hundred. Now that would be funny—that I could be an old lady at fifteen!" She started to laugh but for just a moment remembered how she had once felt old and bruised and—

She shivered, chilled to the core.

"Rose?" Evelyn said.

"Yeah?"

"I'm sure a stream will be fine. For the music."

Rose looked around, noticed the festive decorations, and snapped back cheerfully into pre-party mode. "Selena wants a DJ."

"Selena can hire one, then."

Rose was still wondering about Evelyn. Why hadn't she ever remarried? She never even dated. A couple of years before, a man from her real estate office called for a while. But Evelyn never went out with him, and the calls stopped. "Do you think you'll ever get married again?" Rose asked.

"What? No," Evelyn said. "I've been married."

"What about being in love?"

"I've been in love."

"You make it sound like a driver's test. You take it once and if you pass, you never have to take it again."

"I . . . didn't think I was capable of the depth of feeling I had for your dad. It's highly unlikely I'll feel that way again. And I don't think I want to." Evelyn untangled a skeleton, pushed a button, and watched it float around the room, slowly jiggling its arms and legs. "Not exactly dancing, is it?"

"Why wouldn't you want to?"

Evelyn sighed. "Let's just say my parents didn't set the best example."

Rose got distracted. The blue chair, her dad's favorite place to sit and watch baseball, had been moved. But she and Evelyn hadn't touched the furniture while getting ready for the party.

When Rose caught up with what Evelyn was saying, it was something about being in a house with a storm raging outside and her mother standing at the window, insisting it was a beautiful day.

"But that was nice of her," Rose said. "Maybe it was a beautiful day and you just hadn't noticed. That happened to me when I woke up on Sunday—it was so beautiful out. I'm so glad I noticed it." She didn't mention the red light, so obtrusive again the past couple of mornings, like the wrong kind of alarm clock.

"That's not what I meant—"

"Did you move the blue chair?"

"What?" Evelyn glanced at the blue chair. "I was reading.

The light from outside was bothering me."

"It left a dent in the rug. See? It's saying, 'I was here, don't forget I was here.' It's saying it as loudly as if it could actually talk. It wants to be put back where it belongs."

Evelyn looked down at the spot. The skeleton swooped between them. "Rose, are you happy?"

"Yes, very," Rose replied without hesitation.

"It's what I've always wanted for you."

Rose tucked her hair behind one ear, a move that had already become almost unconscious. "Then you got what you always wanted. Now you, your turn. Are you happy?"

Evelyn looked at her carefully. "Yes and no."

"Meaning—?"

"Meaning, I am if you are."

But Rose had just said she was.

CHAPTER 8

"The thing to remember about cats," Dr. Lola told Rose on Saturday morning, her first day at the animal hospital, "is that you can't hold a cat that doesn't want to be held. Cats are still somewhat wild, much more so than dogs. Dogs are pussycats."

"Dogs are pussycats?"

"But guess what. You can fool a cat, psych her out. That's your weapon. Never mind that a cat can run away if she tries to. She'll stay if you make her think you're in control."

Dr. Lola had given Rose a pale-green smock to wear over her clothes. Rose had spent the morning cleaning out litter pans and refilling bowls with dry food and water. The whole place had a dark, musty scent.

Dr. Lola picked up a black-and-white cat. "This guy is the Great Catsby. Hello, Catsby," she said firmly, pulling the skin on the back of his neck so tight his eyes became slits. "Don't look so alarmed, Rose. When they're kittens, their mothers carry them around like this." Dr. Lola gave Rose's hair a careful look. "That your natural color?"

"I wish!"

"Well, at least you chose a reasonable shade. When I was your age, I dyed mine rainbow stripes. Can you imagine? My parents tried to get mad at me, but they couldn't stop laughing!"

It sounded like Dr. Lola's childhood had been a happy one.

That was when Rose felt it—a trickle of anger that traced a searing path along the inside of her chest.

Then Rose remembered the lady she'd talked to who knew things about her that she was only now discovering for herself, and heard the lady saying in that flat, generic voice, as if joining in the conversation, *There's no anger. It's gone—like a banished king, never to return.* Once again, she was exactly right—why be angry about the fact that Dr. Lola might've had a happy childhood? Rose took a long, deep, calming breath that filled her lungs.

"I bet you looked pretty," Rose said lightly.

"Sweet of you to say. So, you've got him by the neck." Dr. Lola tightened her grip. "You can't lose confidence. Don't go near his mouth or he'll bite you. Wrap your other arm around his legs, like this, so he can't scratch you."

Rose laughed nervously.

"You should be glad we only do cats and dogs here, no exotics—parrots, snakes, ferrets. Now, Catsby needs a shot. He's got kidney problems. Don't worry about the needle." The needle looked about a foot long. "He won't feel it; cats have thick skins." Quickly Dr. Lola let go of his legs, pinched some skin on his back, and stuck the needle right in. After a moment the cat let out a low growl.

"I thought he couldn't feel it."

"It's the medicine; it burns a little." Dr. Lola took the needle out. "Now he needs a pill. Here's how you pill a cat." She popped open the cat's mouth by pinching the corners of his jaw and tossed in a pill overhand, like a pitcher. "See how I'm stroking his throat? He can't help but swallow; it's a reflex. Otherwise he'd spit it right out. Ever try to shove a soggy pill down a cat's throat? Not fun." Then she placed him in a cage.

Dr. Lola asked Rose to take Rouge out for a walk. Unlike Cocoa and Fudge, Rouge walked like a dream. She kept pace with Rose's every step, never budged from her side, and sat obediently at red lights.

It began to snow lightly, an early first snow of the year, little bits of fluff falling to earth and melting without a trace, like they'd never been there at all. Rose wandered through the kids' playground at Belle Heights Park and stood next to the motion-sensor fountain, where large concrete turtles sprayed water in the summer. "My dad used to bring me here," she told Rouge. "He held me up even though that meant his clothes got all wet. Once he ruined a really nice suit. My stepmother wasn't thrilled, but he said it was only a suit and I was having so much fun."

This was one reason people liked dogs, Rose realized. They were such good listeners. Trustworthy, too. She knew Rouge wouldn't tell a soul.

That afternoon a woman named Ms. Brackman stopped in with her cocker spaniel, Candy. Stacey, the receptionist, told Ms. Brackman to please take a seat.

"Candy hates to wait," Ms. Brackman said, not sitting.

"It'll be just a minute," Stacey said.

"Candy doesn't know that. For all Candy knows, it's forever. She's eleven, you know. That's seventy-seven human years. Older than me, and I'm no spring chicken."

"Would you like to wait outside?" Stacey asked her.

"It's snowing!" Ms. Brackman said, though it had already stopped and hadn't stuck. "Do you have any idea how hard it was to get Candy here in the first place?" After waiting for an answer that didn't come, she sat with a thud. "I'm staying put. Candy'll do anything for chicken, broiled, no skin. I always have some in my purse." Candy ate it eagerly and noisily. She had mournful eyes. Maybe that defined the breed, Rose thought, mourning dogs.

"I heard the most fascinating story," Ms. Brackman said, turning her attention to Rose. "There were these two dogs that were always fighting. One day, one of the dogs died. You'd think the other dog would be happy—but no. He went to the site where the dog was buried and dug him up."

"That's awful," Rose said.

"I'm getting to the good part! It turned out the other dog was still alive! He was in a coma, or had fainted. Now you'd think the dogs would become best friends after this, right? Because one dog had saved the other's life? Well, guess again. They went right back to hating each other."

There was silence for a moment.

"I don't think it's true," Stacey said then. "No one would bury a dog that had fainted."

"Or was in a coma," Ms. Brackman corrected her.

"Even so," Stacey said. "When you hold the dog, it's warm, you can feel it breathing. And, what, the dog was buried somewhere out in the open, not in a pet cemetery?"

"It's a reliable story," Ms. Brackman said, drawing herself up and standing. "It came from a highly reliable source. And I might watch my tone, young lady." She walked to Stacey, leaned across the counter, and picked up an index card on Stacey's desk. "What's this?"

"What's what?"

"It's Candy's card, isn't it? It's got a red star on it. With the letters TC, also in red. Look at that, my name's got TCO next to it."

Stacey pulled the card away. "It doesn't mean anything."

"Of course it means something," Ms. Brackman said, "or why go to the trouble of writing it? And it's in *red*."

Stacey was turning red herself.

Rose had never thought of herself as fast on her feet, but the words seemed to tumble out of her. "That red star means the animal is wonderful. Just this morning I heard Dr. Lola talking about Candy. Candy's her favorite."

Ms. Brackman beamed. "That's so true. Candy's everybody's

57

favorite! And the initials—?"

"TC means Terribly Cute." Rose didn't miss a beat. "TCO means Trustworthy, Caring Owner. That means we can count on you to give Candy the right dose of the right medication."

"That's certainly true too," Ms. Brackman said.

Stacey looked gratefully at Rose.

Finally Dr. Lola was ready for Candy, who leaned back heavily and struggled, but Ms. Brackman pulled her along.

"I can't believe she was nosy enough to read the card," Stacey said. "I can't believe she had the nerve to ask about it."

"What do the letters really mean?"

"TC means Typical Cocker. They're overbred and crazy. TCO is Typical Cocker Owner. Draw your own conclusions. The red star means bad dog, watch out. Maybe Candy's a biter."

"Candy—everybody's favorite?"

"The very same."

"What if somebody stole Ms. Brackman's purse? The thief would find—"

"Chicken, broiled, no skin!" Stacey laughed.

Rose laughed too. Despite the age difference, Rose felt an instant connection here, a kindred spirit. Selena and Astrid would like her too; so would Kim. The five of them could do all kinds of fun things together. But what did Stacey like to do?

"Why don't you tell me about yourself?" Rose asked her.

"Well . . . this isn't exactly the time or place."

"Where were you born? How'd you get interested in working with animals? Do you like to go shopping? I'm trying to find a jean jacket, a very particular one. I went to Second Nature four times already, but they never have it."

Stacey just shook her head.

"You can tell me things. I'm a really good listener, contrary to what a certain bio teacher might say. What do you think about when you wake up alone in the middle of the night?"

"What makes you think I wake up alone?"

"Sorry, I didn't mean to get personal. I used to wake up several times a night. Some therapist told me to count backward by threes, that it would make me sleepy, but I got so good at it, it woke me up even more. I could count backward by threes from any random number. Even now I can do it—five-forty-eight, five-forty-five, five-forty-two, five-thirty-nine, see? I went to so many therapists, you wouldn't believe it."

"Rose, this is . . . much too much."

"How so? We're friends!"

"We just met."

"Technically, we met the other day, but it doesn't matter. I'm having a Halloween party tonight. Please come! You don't need a costume. I'm not wearing one. I'd really like to introduce you to my friends. So will you come?"

"What grade are you in, anyway?"

"Tenth."

"Rose, I think I'm a little old for a high school party."

"You never know—you might change your mind. Tell me your number—I'll send you the address." Rose opened her phone. "Don't pay attention to the picture. I keep forgetting to get rid of it. Do you forget to do stuff you know you should do but you just don't do it?"

"I can't really have this conversation right now."

"Later, then?"

"We'll see."

Which sounded too much like what parents say to children when they mean no. She'd always hated it when her dad tried to tell her no.

CHAPTER 9

The party was packed.

"Isn't it fun?" Rose had to shout at Evelyn over the music.

Evelyn smiled briefly, though Rose could tell she wasn't a big fan of parties. She liked quiet evenings, thick books, old movies. Selena had certainly spread the word—there were a lot of kids there Rose didn't know, some she didn't even recognize, who looked like seniors, or older. Stacey would fit right in! Nick Winter hadn't arrived yet. Rose looked around for Kim, who wasn't there either. Skeletons bobbled around overhead; they got tangled in each other's arms, but someone always pulled them down and freed them. Some of the pumpkins glowed, some just flickered, and a few were entirely dark. Rose made her way over to Astrid and Selena and the group inevitably surrounding them.

"You invited Kim, right?" Rose shouted at Selena.

"I said I did, didn't I?" Selena didn't have to shout; her voice was naturally loud.

"She's not here."

"Take it easy, Rose. Maybe I forgot, whatever. I'll invite her now." Selena took out her phone.

Rose, making sure of it, watched over Selena's shoulder as she opened the student directory, and said, "It's so late now. She probably has other plans."

"You're kidding, right?" Astrid said. "We're talking about Kim Garcia." She was wearing a sleeveless black dress with a web design. She pointed to a tattoo of a small black spider slowly crawling on her arm. "It's the real thing, none of that stupid Sün-Fade stuff for me. It's got a three-inch radius."

"Didn't your mother mind?" asked a girl dressed as a cow-girl.

"She's never home to notice. She's in Argentina now, working on husband number nine." Astrid, whose voice was always so low, might've said "five"—which was more likely, Rose thought, though that was still a lot of ex-husbands. Astrid grinned. "I got another tattoo, too. Don't ask where."

Dylan Beck, Nick Winter's best friend, was dressed as a banana. He wrapped an arm around Astrid. "Want to pin the tail on the donkey? You be the donkey and I'll be the tail." He laughed as if this was the height of wit. Astrid pushed him off; she never went out with high school guys. Dylan said to Rose, "Who are you supposed to be, your own mother?"

Rose was wearing an old dress of Evelyn's, the color of fallen leaves. "I'm not in costume," she said, and then thought, *Yes, I am.* Which didn't make any sense.

Selena had on a leather jumpsuit and love beads with a huge peace sign. "So have you seen her yet?" she bellowed at Rose.

"Who?"

"The psychic!"

Rose hadn't even met her. Evelyn had set her up in Rose's room.

"I barely had to say a word," Selena said. "She told me my uncle just died, and that I have a crush on my sister's boyfriend. The psychic knew everything!"

Somebody else said a friend of her mom's had gone to a psychic and uncovered a traumatic episode in her past. "My mom suspects she had memory work done to help her through it," she added.

"What kind of memory work?" asked a girl dressed as a zombie. Retro costumes were big this year, pirates, magicians, ghosts, vampires, along with cowboys and zombies.

"Oh, could be any one of these new things," Selena answered her. "Memory wipe, like cleaning off a blackboard, or a memory replacement of your choice, or a total memory transfer from somebody else. I saw a bunch of videos. This one woman said her sister went from hating her husband to loving him like they'd just met."

"Yeah, I saw a few of those videos," Rose said. "Interesting but kinda crazy, you know?"

The girl in the cowgirl dress shrieked—a skeleton foot was tangled in her hair. Another girl was helping untangle it, but not before taking a picture. "Don't you *dare* make a video out of that," the cowgirl said.

"It reminds me of Hypno-Friends," said the zombie girl. "What a disaster! You got hypnotized into remembering a wonderful best friend you had when you were a kid. People said it made their childhood memories a million times better. But it turns out people would believe the best friends really existed and then try to find them, hiring detectives, placing ads—and then some creeps would answer the ads, saying yeah, it's me, your best buddy, and oh, by the way, I need money. They had to shut the whole thing down."

"I spoke to the psychic," Astrid said. "She didn't uncover any buried trauma or a Hypno-Friend, but she told me things I've never told anyone." She shook back her long, glistening, skeleton-free hair. "And I'm not repeating any of it."

"Darcy Franzen's in there now," Selena said. "She's probably hearing, 'You will take home a guy tonight.' With her parents in Europe, doesn't take a psychic to get that right!" She jabbed a sharp elbow into Rose's ribs. "What's wrong with your face?"

"Nothing." Rose realized she was rubbing her jaw and stopped. That strange pain hadn't gone away yet. She headed for her room just as Darcy Franzen was leaving—practically in tears.

"My personal life is none of her damn business," Darcy said.

"What'd she say?" Rose asked her.

"Oh my God." Darcy waved Rose away.

Rose felt bad; kids were supposed to be having fun.

Rose's room was surprisingly quiet behind the closed door. She sat and faced the psychic—a tanned woman all in white, cinnamon-colored hair in many braids with colorful beads that clicked. Well, she certainly dressed the part. She spoke in a hushed tone, but her voice filled the room. "You live here," she said.

"How'd you know?"

"By the way you entered. This is your room and you didn't need to look around. May I take your hand?"

She held Rose's hand in her rough fingers. Rose smelled peppermint. A long time passed, or maybe it only seemed that way. The beads clicked. Selena had made it sound like the details of your life would come spilling out.

"Well?" said Rose.

"Perhaps you could tell me about yourself."

"I thought it was the other way around."

"Please," the psychic said.

Rose cleared her throat. "Okay, I'm a tenth grader at Belle Heights High. I live with my stepmother, Evelyn."

"Do you two get along?"

"Lately, yes." Rose hadn't known she would say "lately" and instantly wished she could take it back, rub it out.

"Lately? Since when?"

"This whole week has been great."

"Before this week?"

"Well, I was kind of moody," Rose said. She caught sight of a bald stuffed elephant on her bed. So embarrassing, that kids saw that when they came into her room. She should've hidden it away in the closet.

"Do you have friends?"

"Of course. I'm very close to a girl I've known since I was a kid. She's supposed to be here. She lives in Belle Heights Tower, a hop, skip, and jump away—my dad used to say stuff like that—but another friend of mine forgot to invite her . . . well, maybe not forgot, and that's wrong, isn't it, when you say you're going to do something and then you don't? Sometimes it's *really* wrong. I mean—"

Rose stopped short. Why was she doing all the talking?

The psychic paused too. "Where is your father?"

"He died when I was eight."

"And your mother?"

"She died when I was a baby."

"I'm so sorry."

This whole conversation was heading in the wrong direction. Why such an emphasis on the past? What about the future?

"Dear girl, I should be sensing something in you, even years after such loss. The work of mourning."

Rose had to smile—it sounded like school service. "I'm over it. I'm very happy."

But it was as if the psychic wasn't listening. "It's as if you're not here."

Rose felt her throat tighten. "So, where am I?"

"Somewhere else."

Rose couldn't believe it. What was she talking about?

"I'm truly sorry. You may send in the next person."

Rose went back to the party, telling herself she didn't believe in psychics any more than she believed in zombies or Hypno-Friends. She started dancing, watching the other kids and copying their movements, hoping she didn't look like one of the bobbling skeletons.

Finally—there was Nick Winter. He looked spectacular, dressed as a pirate with an eye patch. Rose went right up to him; instantly he grabbed her and held her close.

"Hey, it's farmer girl," he said.

She noticed, among lots of other thrilling things, that at over six feet he was the perfect height for her. "I'm here," she said, and didn't care how it sounded. "I'm here."

"You don't have to convince me." Nick grinned. There was that diamond in his front tooth.

"Did that hurt, putting a diamond in there?"

"No nerves in the teeth. You like it?"

It sparkled like a star. "Yes."

"I like *you*, farmer girl," he slurred. He tilted his head at the music. "Yeah, great song!" He kissed her. Her first kiss! But she tasted something musty and sharp on his breath. He couldn't have been smoking or drinking here, not with Evelyn keeping close watch. But maybe that was why he'd arrived so late. This wasn't her idea of what a perfect first kiss should be, far from it. But Nick liked her. He'd said so.

By the time everyone went home, it was nearly two. At the door, Selena's elbow managed to poke Rose's ribs again. "Look at you, getting all up close and personal with Nick."

Rose couldn't help grabbing hold of that elbow of Selena's. "You're not upset or anything?"

"Oh God, no. A bunch of us are getting together for brunch at noon tomorrow, or should I say later today? At Stella Dallas, that place next to the old movie house. You know where that is?"

"I'll find it," Rose said.

"We can plan the next party!"

CHAPTER 10

Rose had never been to Stella Dallas or to the old movie house, You Must Remember This, which showed twentieth-century films and didn't even have a holo-screen. She figured she'd look up the route on her phone but then forgot her phone; still, she found her way easily, even while walking along unfamiliar streets that had names instead of numbers—Belle Circle, Forest Glen, Fragrant Meadows—bordered by tall trees filled with chattering sparrows. Why couldn't these birds nest on Mrs. Moore's windowsill instead of ones that sounded so sad all the time? Rose had slept deeply and felt great—well, good. The red light had been there when she woke up and hadn't faded until she started brushing her teeth, which was definitely something new. And she couldn't help saying to Evelyn on her way out the door, "I'm sorry we hired that psychic. I said I'd pay for her, but what a waste."

"She wouldn't accept payment," Evelyn had said.

"What—why not?"

"Something about an incomplete reading."

Rose shrugged this off. "I'll be home right after brunch." As if brunch was something Rose did every Sunday and this wasn't her first time.

Stella Dallas was a coffee shop plastered with movie posters from years gone by. Rose knew some of the famous names, Marilyn Monroe and Jack Nicholson, and didn't recognize others, Joel McCrea, Molly Ringwald. She took off her coat, one of Evelyn's—wool, tweedy, with fake fur around the collar—and became the seventh person to squeeze into a booth meant for six, leaving her half on, half off the padded bench next to Dylan Beck, who wasn't giving an inch, and a couple of guys she didn't know. Across from her were Selena, Astrid, and a girl she didn't know either. *There's no room for me here,* she thought. *I could've just been someone passing by,* and then had to remind herself that of course that wasn't true; Selena had specially invited her only hours before.

And Selena immediately focused on her, leaning across the table. "Such a cool party! Everyone's asking, how about another one next weekend? You can get a DJ then. It's a lot more fun than a stream."

"I know something a lot more fun than a stream," Dylan said.

"Shut up," Astrid said. She had deep shadows beneath her eyes.

Dylan reached for her, which knocked open a bottle of ketchup on the Formica tabletop. No one moved to clean up the spill, so Rose used her napkin to wipe it up. "I heard a really strange story yesterday, at Belle Heights Animal Hospital."

"I know that place," Dylan said. "They put my cat under for an operation and she never woke up."

Rose thought that sounded awful. Never getting a chance to say good-bye. "It's not that kind of story. There were these dogs that hated each other. One day, one of them died—"

"Don't talk about that!" Selena cried. "I had a schnorgi. I loved her so much. She died last year."

"What's a schnorgi?" asked the girl Rose didn't know.

"Half schnauzer, half corgi, and all a-dog-able."

"That's the stupidest thing I have ever heard from you," Astrid said.

Selena looked like she might cry.

"Don't be such a baby," Astrid said.

"You're calling *me* stupid! Meanwhile *she's* telling us some horrible story about dead dogs!"

"That's just it," Rose said. "The dog wasn't dead—it was alive the whole time, and somehow the other dog knew it and dug him up. But even after that, they still hated each other. Actually, I don't like the ending to this story; this experience should've changed them on the deepest level, brought them closer together—"

"Stop! I miss my schnorgi." Selena held her hands over her ears.

Rose remembered doing that as a kid. Holding her hands over her ears, pressing hard, shutting her eyes tight—anything to blot out the world, make it go away.

Across the room, near a poster for a movie called *Ball of Fire*, Rose saw a girl with a long, ropy braid down her back, sitting at the crowded counter. Kim was here! Rose could bring Kim over to the table and squeeze her in, too. But there were older people on either side of Kim, maybe an aunt and uncle.

"I was meaning to tell you," one of the guys next to Rose said. "Your mom is *hot*."

A waiter came to their table. Rose looked up to see a short kid in a black T-shirt and black jeans, with frizzy, curly hair and bushy eyebrows that were almost a unibrow—the kid from the cafeteria scanner. Kim had mentioned his name—what was it? "It's . . . you," she said.

"It's me, all right."

"You work here, too?"

"My parents own the place. Weekends are busy, so I help out."

"I guess they like movies, huh?"

"That's an understatement. My mom's from Korea and my dad's from the Dominican Republic. Their families thought they couldn't possibly have anything in common, but they did."

Everyone else at the table was ignoring them, talking to one another. Rose gestured to the poster across the room. "What's *Ball of Fire*?"

"A screwball comedy from 1941, with Gary Cooper and the lovely Barbara Stanwyck."

Rose remembered that he'd told her she looked like Barbara

Stanwyck. "What's it about?"

"There's this nightclub singer who has to hide out because her mobster boyfriend is in trouble with the law. She ends up in a house with eight professors writing an encyclopedia—"

"Can we order, already?" Astrid asked.

"In a second," Rose said. "I want to hear this. Go on."

"These professors never really leave the house, so she helps them write part of their encyclopedia about the slang of the day. It's actually based on 'Snow White and the Seven Dwarves.'"

"No kidding! My dad used to read that to me all the time. I practically had it memorized. But you said there were eight professors, not seven?"

"Gary Cooper is the prince."

"Oh." He had amazing eyes, she noticed, brown with flecks of green.

"I'm named after Gary Cooper. Though I think he was a lot taller."

"Your name is Gary?" But that sounded wrong.

"Cooper," he said.

"I'll have cranberry pancakes," Astrid broke in. "Double-shot latte. No, triple."

Cooper took the rest of their orders; Rose got the steel-cut oatmeal. As Cooper left, he told Rose, "Sometimes they show that movie next door. Keep an eye out."

"I will," she said.

"I would *never*," Selena said. "I only see holo-films. I like how you feel in the middle of everything. Though they make my cousin throw up."

"Where's Nick?" Rose said.

They all looked at one another.

"He had a late night," Dylan said. "He's sleeping it off."

Selena's fist came down on the table, knocking over the ketchup bottle again. "Can't keep a secret, can you?"

"What're you talking about?" Dylan said. "I didn't say anything!"

Rose agreed. It was Selena who was giving things away. "He went out with someone after the party, didn't he," Rose said, stating it as a fact.

"Darcy Franzen," Selena said.

Rose looked at the splotch of ketchup and didn't clean it up.

"Are you seriously upset?" Selena said. "I mean, it's Nick, so . . ."

Rose glanced over at Kim. The people on either side of her had left—they hadn't been an aunt and uncle, after all. Kim was alone. "I have to talk to someone."

"If you call Nick—" Selena said, alarmed.

"You always called him," Astrid said, "and he always denied everything."

"Nick never cheated on me!" Selena said.

"Keep telling yourself that," Astrid said.

"I'm not calling Nick," Rose said. "I don't even have my phone." She headed over to Kim.

* * *

Kim was just finishing a stack of blueberry pancakes. She had on a paisley sweatshirt dress with metal clasps in the front. "Hey," she said, offering Rose half an orange juice stick. "Want a bite?"

"I'm sitting with them." Rose pointed to her table.

Kim glanced and made a face. She said, "You see who works here?"

"Cooper," Rose said. "As in Gary Cooper."

"Ha, I didn't know that! Makes sense, though." Kim waved an arm at the movie posters.

"I wanted you at my party. I know you only got a last-minute invite."

"I couldn't have gone anyway. Had to babysit. This family had a crazy basset hound. I was told it was in a locked room, but it got out somehow and chased me into the kids' room. I was in there until midnight, with the dog outside, howling. The kids thought it was hilarious. How was the party?"

"Really great but—Nick Winter? He hung out with me, and I just heard he got together after with Darcy Franzen."

"No big loss. Maybe for Darcy Franzen, but not for you." Kim pointed her thumb at the poster for *Ball of Fire*. "You do look like Barbara Stanwyck."

"There was a psychic at the party. Everybody said she was amazing, but she wouldn't tell me anything. She kept asking me questions about when I was little. Don't you think that's weird?"

Kim shrugged.

"I was spoiled," Rose said, "wasn't I? My dad spoiled me."

A sort of sad smile spread across Kim's face. "Your dad was

a single parent practically since you were born. He did the best he could. He kinda had a hard time saying no to you."

"I was a brat," Rose said with conviction. Which meant that everything that had happened had been just what you'd expect, right? Her dad had been the way he was because she didn't have a mom, and later she'd gotten sort of moody for a time because her dad was gone, too. It wasn't that complicated, certainly nothing to dwell on.

"Yeah, you were the brat of Belle Heights," Kim said. "I loved you anyway." She hesitated. "I still love you."

"Oh, I love you, too!" Rose beamed at her.

"So why are you with them?"

Rose kept smiling. "We could all be friends, though. Don't you think? We could do so many fun things together."

Kim said that wasn't going to happen—and called her by her old name.

"It's *Rose*. Don't I look like a Rose? The lipstick, the hair?" She tucked some hair behind one ear. "I know I don't have the exact right jean jacket—but I'll find it soon."

Kim got up. "Come over later. Doesn't matter when. Just—drop by."

Rose went back to her table, having to push to reclaim even her tiny portion of the bench. She half listened to a story about some girl who got her lips puffed and they looked *horrible*. She glanced out the window at stark branches against a swirling gray sky, clouds all smeared as if someone had tried to rub them out.

That was when she saw it—Forget-Me-Not.

There was a three-story brick building across the street, not the kind of building you'd ever look twice at. On the second floor, right above a cell phone store, were the words, not very big, in plain black on one of the windows—in the same lettering as on that receipt she'd found last weekend, for sixteen hundred dollars. Evelyn had said it was a flower shop. It didn't look anything like a flower shop. There weren't any flowers.

She clasped her hand to her jaw. What had been a dull ache had turned to searing pain.

"What's the matter?" Selena said. "It's Nick and Darcy, isn't it?"

Rose stood. Her half-eaten oatmeal looked thick and soggy as wet cement. She placed some money on the table.

"Thanks. I may need that if I can't find any cash," Selena said.

"It's the tip."

"For that stupid waiter who wouldn't shut up?" Astrid said. "I ought to tell the owners to fire him."

Rose picked up the tip. "I'll give it to him myself."

"The party?" Selena said. "Next week? I'll tell everybody."

At the door, Cooper came to Rose's side. "Are you all right?"

"My jaw really hurts," she said, practically hunched over.

"How'd you hurt it?"

"I don't know."

He just looked at her. "Hey, if you need to lie down, there's a room in the back with a couch. Do you want me to call someone to pick you up?"

He was really nice. "Cooper," she said, and insisted he take the tip, and by mistake told him her old name, maybe because Kim had just said it, and realized she felt better. "It's nice to actually meet you."

"Nice to actually meet you, too."

He stuck out his hand. Such an old-fashioned gesture. She took it. And didn't let go. They just held hands.

"Would you want to hang out sometime?"

"I don't know—there's this guy . . ." She shook her head. "Well, I guess not, really. I might've set a world record for the shortest relationship ever."

"I bet I beat it. One time I took a girl to the movies. Her old boyfriend was on line behind us, and by the time I bought the tickets, they were back together."

She smiled.

"Now that's a real smile," he said.

She pointed across the street. "You see that place, Forget-Me-Not? What is it?"

"No idea. I never noticed it before."

Exactly. It was meant not to be noticed.

"Are you heading up there?" he asked her.

"Yes. No. I'm going . . . somewhere else. To the Bronx Global Conservation Center."

"You mean the zoo?"

"I mean the zoo."

"Mm-hmm." Cooper looked deep in thought. "The rush here is winding down, and I haven't been to the zoo in . . . ever."

"Really? You've got to see the gorillas!" She gave his hand a tug.

"Let me get my jacket. I'd love to see the gorillas."

CHAPTER 11

An old express bus left Belle Heights every hour on the hour in the direction of the zoo and returned to Belle Heights every hour on the half hour. Rose and Cooper found seats together; Rose settled into the cushy fabric lining, so unlike the plastic seats on hydro-buses. Cooper had on a bulky shearling jacket, which, since it was slightly too big for him, made Rose feel like she was sitting next to an overstuffed pillow.

Neither one said anything down several hilly, curving streets of Belle Heights.

Rose spoke first. "Wish I had my phone with me. I've got a great song on it. 'Changes,' by David Bowie."

"Ch-ch-ch-ch-changes," Cooper sang, very badly. "Here, try this one."

He took out his phone, found the song he wanted, and held it to her ear. It was a short song with a simple, quiet, lilting tune, and the words—well, they took her breath away.

It seems we stood and talked like this before
We looked at each other in the same way then,
But I can't remember where or when.

Some things that happen for the first time,
Seem to be happening again.
And so it seems that we have met before,
And laughed before, and loved before,
But who knows where or when.

"You like it?" Cooper asked her.

"More than that. I'm crazy about it."

"It's called 'Where or When,' from a Broadway show almost a hundred years old."

But it could have been written that day and sung for the first time by the person sitting behind them on the bus. It felt that immediate and timeless.

Cooper started talking, mostly about his family. He had two older sisters, Ava and Ginger; one was a geneticist, and the other was an engineer who built suspension bridges. "That takes all the pressure off me. I can do—whatever." Which turned out to be writing and filming his own science-fiction movie. "Everything will be exactly the way it is now, except for one specific thing."

"And what's that?"

"Haven't gotten quite that far yet."

Rose laughed. She liked Cooper's voice, easy and gentle.

Back in the diner, she'd liked his eyes, and how he'd held her hand.

Things were starting to add up here.

When they got off the bus, the wind was sharply colder. Rose huddled inside her coat and pressed her face into the collar.

"Cold?" Cooper said. "I can give you my jacket."

"No, I'm okay." She remembered something from long ago. "That's what Kim used to do for me, when we were kids."

"That sounds like Kim, all right. Giving you the coat off her back."

"She was always too warm—she thinks her body temperature is naturally about two degrees hotter than everybody else's. When she got a fever, it went up to something scary crazy, like a hundred and four."

They made their way to the Congo Gorilla Forest. But instead of letting them go right into the building, a man at the gate said they had to pay extra for it.

"This isn't included in the price of admission?" Rose said.

"Only if you have the Total Experience Package."

"That sounds like one of those you-gotta-have-it ads," Cooper said, and deepened his voice like an announcer: "With the Total Experience Package, you'll have it all, perfect marriage, perfect job, perfect life!"

Rose ignored Cooper. This thing about the Total Experience Package was bothering her. "Is this something new?" she asked the man.

"Nope, been going on for years and years." He continued to scan ticket stubs and let people in as he spoke.

"I was here last week. Nobody asked for money for the Congo Gorilla Forest."

"Then somebody was asleep on the job. You must've seen signs for it. They're everywhere."

Well, sure they were. *Now.*

"It's only three dollars," Cooper said. "I'll treat you. I just got a nice tip."

The entrance consisted of a long, skinny, zigzag hall that felt like a maze with no choice of paths that kept pushing you forward. Rose had no memory of this, either. It was very crowded, shoulder to shoulder. Last week, it hadn't been nearly so busy, and the other visitors were chatty and friendly, the kids smiling and laughing. Now a lady taking a photo shoved Rose aside and didn't even apologize, and a kid wailed for his mom, who said, irritably, "Stop it, I'm right here!"

Rose and Cooper finally managed to reach the floor-to-ceiling windows looking onto the gorilla habitat outside. Rose couldn't believe it. Several gorillas sat calmly gazing at the crowd, but there was one—a huge one—glaring at people as if wanting to tear them apart, if not for this thick glass.

"You were right about the gorillas," Cooper said. "They're amazing."

But what happened to the tender gorilla cradling her baby?

Rose broke away from Cooper, pushing past people, looking for someone who worked here. She spotted a woman all in khaki, holding a clipboard. "What's wrong with her?" Rose asked.

"What's wrong with who?"

Wasn't it obvious? "The gorilla."

The woman grinned. "That's one of the famous Pattycake's many descendants. Her name is Candy."

"You're wrong. Candy's a cocker spaniel."

"Well, this girl's nearly twenty and her name has always been Candy."

The air in the room was starting to feel close and stifling. Rose felt sweat gather on the back of her neck. "I was here last week. There was a mother gorilla and a baby."

"No babies at the moment. Just Candy and her almost fully grown children."

"She looked loving and kind."

The woman glanced down at her clipboard and scribbled something. "Candy's only got two expressions—mean and meaner."

"She was keeping the baby safe and sound."

The woman looked up; clearly she had work to do, but she wasn't hurrying Rose along. "Maybe you saw a photograph of a gorilla. Ever hear of Koko? She had a kitten she adored."

"I'm not confusing anything with anything." Rose pointed at the gorilla. "I know what I saw."

"No need to raise your voice, sweetheart," the woman said softly.

Rose turned away.

Now she noticed plants in large tubs at the edge of the exhibit, and her eyes widened. Last week they'd been lush and green. Now the long, heart-shaped leaves were scarred and brown, the stalks all tangled. How was this possible? These plants had been neglected for far longer than a week. Something had to be done—right away. She plunged both hands into the dirt.

"Hey, you can't do that!" a guard yelled.

"These plants need to be moved." Rose scratched at the soil. "There's a rooftop garden on Belle Heights Tower. It'll be the perfect place—they can heal and grow."

"Girlie, knock it off! Do I need to call security?"

Her hands were smeared, the fingernails black.

"You have to leave," the guard said, "now."

"Will you make sure someone takes care of the plants?"

"Yeah, yeah, sure."

She didn't believe him.

Cooper rushed to her side. "I couldn't find you. Where'd you go?" He looked at her hands. "What happened to you?"

"The people who work here don't know anything about anything."

"Come on—let's get those hands washed." He led her to a fountain. He turned on the water and held her hands under the stream.

She watched as rivers of dirt ran down the drain. "I could go to the ladies' room, use the sink."

"I think I'd better keep an eye on you." Cooper dried her

hands on the sleeve of his jacket, which got dirty.

"Oh, your jacket," she said.

"Not a problem."

She looked down. "My hands look younger now."

"You mean cleaner." Cooper was starting to sound worried.

Outside, the icy winds were even more chilling because Rose had gotten kind of sweaty inside. "I don't understand," she said. "Last week it wasn't this cold." She thought hard, frowning. "There was no weather at all."

Cooper actually took her arm. "Enough zoo for today," he said, leading her to the bus stop. "And, um, by the way, one thing you can count on is there's always weather—it's breezy, or raining, or the clouds are hazy, or there are no clouds at all and the sky's a brilliant blue. You know, even if the air feels like 'room temperature,' that's still weather, right?"

"I'm telling you how it was" was all Rose would say.

She was quiet on the bus home. She leaned her head against the window and stared out at rows of houses with patches of lawns surrounded by chain-link fences. Some lawns were well manicured; some were scruffy; some had wildflowers at the edges, bursting at the seams. Out of the corner of her eye, she noticed that Cooper kept glancing over at her. His coat was taking up half her seat.

After a while, Cooper cleared his throat. "Hey, don't take this the wrong way, but . . . were you really at the zoo last week?"

"Of course!"

"I'm not so sure. All signs point to no on the Magic Eight

Ball, if you know what I mean." He hesitated. "My timing might be really bad here—I kinda hate to bring this up, but maybe your memory got tampered with. I mean, that happens these days. Do you ever think that?"

Rose shook her head.

"Hey, it might explain a few things."

She kept shaking her head. There wasn't a big enough *no* when it came to something like this.

"How can you be so sure?"

"Because I would never do such a thing, never. If you knew me at all, you'd know that."

"Well, I'm getting to know you, right?" Cooper looked at her intently. "You've changed a lot, your hair, your clothes, your personality—"

She smiled brightly. The explanation for all that came to her easily. "I'm growing up."

"Hey, I'm just saying, maybe it wasn't your idea at all, maybe somebody arranged it for you. It wouldn't be the first time, from what I've read."

That stopped her cold. The receipt, seeing Forget-Me-Not—the flower place that couldn't possibly be a flower place. Had something been done to her memory there? She couldn't help thinking, *If anyone did that to me—well, I don't hate people, but I'd be very unhappy with that person forever.*

Back in Belle Heights, Rose told Cooper what she was about to do. Cooper, looking even smaller in his big coat, suggested it might be a good idea to go home instead. She shook her head again. Then he offered to accompany her, but Rose said she had to do this alone. She knew, without once looking behind her, that he was watching until she disappeared from sight.

Outside Forget-Me-Not, sparrows chattered loudly in what sounded like a ferocious argument. What were they so upset about? Rose pressed the buzzer next to a camera lens.

"May I help you?" said a woman's voice that was flat and generic.

Rose just stood there, frozen.

"Yes?" said the voice. "I can see that you're still there."

She managed to get the words out: "Is this a flower shop?"

There was a pause. "No."

"What is it, then?"

"A stationery store."

"Can I see some stationery?"

"You're not trade. We only sell to trade."

"I'm trade." Rose didn't know what it meant.

There was another pause. A hydro-bus sped by and hit a bump with a loud clunk. "Appointment only," the lady said finally, and: "We're about to close."

"I know your voice," Rose said. "The kinds of things you say."

There was a sigh. "Oh, for heaven's sake." The voice was suddenly impatient. "This is Rose Hartel, isn't it? The hair's different—it threw me. Listen, go home, Rose. You never came here."

"I'm not leaving," Rose said, with a flash of what felt like a long-familiar streak of stubbornness.

Another sigh.

The door buzzed. Rose opened it and stepped inside.

PART 2

The Glass Coffin

CHAPTER 12

"It feels like dead man's finger!"

That was Clara's excuse, why she wouldn't hold hands with her stepmother when they were crossing the street. It was something her dad had shown her. If you put your palm flat up against someone else's palm and, with your other hand, rub the outsides of both index fingers, your finger feels numb, like your hand isn't yours anymore.

"Her hand does not feel like dead man's finger," her dad would tell her. His voice always sounded like he was smiling, even when he wasn't. He was tall like a tree and had blue eyes with heavy lids, so sometimes Clara couldn't see them. "You hurt her feelings."

"She doesn't have feelings."

"Clara! That's not my girl!"

"Read," Clara would say, as she did every night, asking to hear the Brothers Grimm fairy tale "Little Snow-white"—that was its proper title, with the word "Little" and a hyphen between "Snow" and "white." Of course, Clara, at eight, could read it herself, but this was something she and her dad had always done, way before he met someone and married again. When he read, Clara always held tight to the elephant that had been her mother's favorite childhood toy, loved so hard its fur was gone. If her room ever caught fire, this was the prized possession Clara would rescue.

These were the best times, hearing the story at night, no matter what might've gone wrong during the day. On that particular brisk September afternoon, her dad had taken her to the zoo. But Clara found animals so alien—they couldn't talk, so how did you know what they were thinking?—especially the nocturnal creatures at the back of the House of Primates, in an exhibit dark as night. Ugly bats hung upside down and a weird thing called a slow loris had eyes as big as saucers. A woman who fed purple grapes to shrieking monkeys told Clara what "nocturnal" meant, though Clara hadn't asked.

"Phil, she's got to get some sleep. She's got school tomorrow," her stepmother said, standing now in Clara's doorway, arms folded, a stern expression on her face, dark-blue eyes focused like a laser on the scene before her. She wore one of those dumb kimonos she always had on at home, black and white, tied at the waist, and she had that long hair, thick as vines. What had her stepmother been doing, before trying to ruin story time for Clara? Probably reading a book so thick the title fit across the spine instead of down it, or watching an old black-and-white movie. Clara didn't understand that. Movies were supposed to be in color. Life was in color, wasn't it? Clara didn't understand anything about her stepmother.

"Read," Clara said again.

"Phil, she's had such a long day at the zoo."

"Clara didn't like it," her dad said. "Just like you."

No, it wasn't at all the same, Clara was sure, even if they both happened to feel the same way about something.

"I'm not a fan of zoos, it's true," her stepmother said, unfolding her arms. "I know they're all ecological and environmental and animal conscious and all that. Still, I don't like to see animals in cages. Humane cages, but cages."

Which meant her reason wasn't the same after all.

"Time to call it a night," her stepmother urged him, still in the doorway, tugging on a gold necklace with a heart-shaped pendant, a gift from Clara's dad. The stepmother wore no other jewelry except for a thin, delicate wedding band. They'd gotten married just that spring, and by a clerk at city hall. The ceremony, her dad had told her, took all of five minutes. "She likes things quiet," her dad had said. "No big shindig for her." Clara had never known her mom, who died so long ago, but there were pictures, including a large one in the living room, where she was laughing. Her dad said of her, "She was so much *fun*." The stepmother wasn't.

"Daddy, don't stop reading," Clara pleaded. "The Queen killed Snow-white after she failed three times." Clara kept careful count. First the Queen ordered the huntsman to kill

Snow-white, but he took pity on her and wouldn't do it. Then the Queen disguised herself as an old woman selling lace, and tied Snow-white up tightly in a lace bodice, but Snow-white was with the seven dwarves by then, and they unlaced her. Then the Queen disguised herself again and created a poison comb that she put in Snow-white's hair; again the dwarves saved her, removing the comb. Finally, again in disguise, the Queen tempted Snow-white into eating a poisoned apple. The dwarves were at a loss and pronounced her dead.

"But she's not dead, not really," Clara's dad said. "She's in a kind of trance."

"Can she see?"

"Her eyes are closed."

"If she opens her eyes?"

"She's in a glass coffin. Things would look far away, blurred."

"Like clouds?"

"Something like that."

"Can she hear?"

"Sounds would be muffled, too."

"Like when you're under water? In the tub I can stick my whole head under and hold my breath."

"She asks these questions so she doesn't have to go to sleep," her stepmother broke in, still in the doorway, no closer. Sometimes Clara thought there was an invisible barrier there, keeping her out. Which was *good*.

"She's always been full of questions," her dad said, sounding proud.

"Stubborn," her stepmother said.

"Strong willed."

"How does it end?" Clara asked, of course knowing exactly how it ended.

But it was her stepmother who said, "Snow-white's in the glass coffin a long, long time. A prince falls in love with her on sight and takes her back to his castle, and on the bumpy ride home the piece of apple in her throat comes unstuck and she wakes up and they get married. Strange ending, though. At the wedding, the Queen is forced to put on iron slippers that have been heated by fire, and dance until she dies. Whose idea was that? Snow-white's?"

"Never. Snow-white is *good*." Still, it worried Clara. What was Snow-white like deep down, where nobody could see?

"Phil," her stepmother said, "if she doesn't get enough sleep, she'll be a wreck tomorrow."

Clara hated those little comments, which were supposed to be helpful and were anything but. Clara knew her stepmother thought she was spoiled, always reminding her to say "please" and "thank you." And there was that time, in Belle Heights Park, when Clara wanted her dad to hold her up over the spraying turtle fountain, even if that meant his special-occasion suit got ruined. Or the time when Clara begged for a stuffed unicorn that was way overpriced and then left it on the bus on the trip home. That was an accident! The worst was when Clara needed special markers for a school project, creating a cover for a made-up book, and she'd forgotten to get them on the way home; she went into a panic that night and sent her dad out, and he had to go to three different places before finding exactly the right ones (not too thick, not too thin). Her stepmother had wanted Clara to tell the teacher she needed an extra day, but Clara couldn't stand to be late, especially knowing that Kim had gotten hers done the day *before*. Kim's book was called *The Birds of Belle Heights*, which was mostly pigeons, but she'd drawn them beautifully. Not that Clara was jealous of her best friend; they'd been inseparable since preschool; but she wanted her own book, *Colorful Cupcakes*, to be beautiful, too.

"We're almost at the end," her dad said now.

Her stepmother sighed and left the doorway.

Her dad read the rest of the story, and Snow-white was happy for the rest of her days. That was the ending Clara liked, when people were happy for the rest of their days. It never said how many days, but Clara assumed it was a great big number, not like what her mother had had.

"You'll read again tomorrow?" Clara said.

"If you're game."

"I'm not a game!"

"Just an expression. It means if you're willing." He grinned and his eyes crinkled.

"I don't like it when I can't see your eyes."

He opened them really wide. "Better?"

She didn't much like that, either.

He clicked off the lamp on the little table next to her bed.

Clara hugged the elephant. "Leave it on."

He clicked it back on. "If the story scares you—"

"I'm not scared." But maybe she was. Her dad always said "Snow-white" was only a make-believe story and could never happen in real life, but Clara wasn't so sure. Snow-white's mother was dead. So was Clara's. Snow-white's father remarried, as had Clara's. The Queen gazed in the enchanted mirror and wanted to know who was the fairest in the land. Clara's stepmother—she looked in the mirror too, pushing back her hair to study her forehead, her arms and legs, even in between her fingers and toes. For hours, it seemed to Clara, who watched from behind the big blue armchair in the living room.

"I think you're frightened," her dad said quietly.

"I don't like it when Snow-white gets lost in the woods. What if she gets eaten by animals?" She didn't want to admit to the other stuff.

"Are you afraid of getting lost?"

"Maybe."

"You'll never be lost as long as I'm here," he promised her. "I will keep you safe and sound."

Clara didn't know what it meant to be "sound," but if it was anything like "safe," it was fine with her. "Go on," she said.

"We're done for tonight, love."

"No, I mean you can leave now."

Clara lay in a pool of light surrounded by dark edges.

CHAPTER 13

Only a couple of months later, on a cold but brilliantly sunny November morning, her stepmother came into her room and gently shook her awake. "I have terrible, terrible news," she said. "I can't think of any way to say it except to say it."

But Clara already knew her dad was dead. What other news could be so terrible, terrible? The smell of lavender—her stepmother's soap, so sticky sweet—made Clara sick to her stomach. The sun's glare off the heart-shaped pendant hurt her eyes.

"Phil was in the kitchen last night. He had what's called a heart attack," her stepmother said. "An ambulance came. I went to the hospital with them while Mrs. Moore from upstairs sat here in case you woke up."

Clara hadn't heard a thing, or even stirred in her bed. She would never again sleep so heavily, or through the night, or without her bedside lamp on.

"I'm so sorry," her stepmother said. "There was nothing the doctors could do."

Clara shut her eyes tight, put her hands over her ears, and pressed hard. Oh, her stepmother was evil. Evil Lynn, Clara would call her from now on; Evil Lynn—bearer of terrible, terrible news. Clara vowed on the spot never to talk to Evil Lynn again, or only when she absolutely had to, and never about her dad, not one word.

There was a crowded service. Kim and her parents came, and lots of other kids from school and their parents. Kim had long hair that glowed with light. She put her arms around Clara, and Clara gave her a big hug. But then Kim said, "Good thing your dad remarried." Clara couldn't believe she'd said that— Kim knew how Clara felt about Evil Lynn. Come to think of it, Clara realized, every time she had said something mean about her stepmother, Kim had said, "She's not so bad," or "Your dad seems really happy with her." Clara had always thought it was just Kim trying to seem grown-up by saying things that sounded mature, nothing to pay much attention to. But now those remarks made Clara question her choice of best friend.

Clara wriggled out of Kim's grasp and said, "You better sit far away from me. I'm getting sick and don't want you to catch it."

Clara didn't know most of the people there. Her dad's friends from the TV production company showed up, and there were a lot of them—camera operators, sound mixers, dolly grips, boom operators. Some made a point of telling Clara what a nice guy her dad had been and how much he'd loved her. Others were sobbing, some loudly, some quietly; still others sat in silence. It was like they were demonstrating many ways for Clara to feel. But Clara began to feel something else. She could see and hear, but everything seemed distant, muted, as if she were behind glass, like Snow-white in the glass coffin. It was almost pleasant. This was a place she could stay, like Snow-white, for a long, long time.

Several months after Clara's dad died, Evil Lynn took Clara to a psychologist. He had wispy hair and thick black glasses.

"When someone you love dies, there is no right or wrong way to react," he told Clara.

Clearly Evil Lynn thought differently, or why drag Clara here?

"You are angry," he said. "Every child is angry at the parent who died. How could your father have done such a thing, leaving you like that?"

Clara was well aware that her dad had done such a thing. *I will keep you safe and sound,* he'd said. He'd broken that promise, big-time.

"You are terrified, the terror of a child who fears she can't survive. Such feelings may intensify as the anniversary approaches," he said.

What feelings? There were no feelings in the glass coffin.

"Why don't you hit the couch with the noodle?" He picked up the noodle—a long, lime-green Styrofoam thing.

"I don't want to hit the couch with the noodle."

"Why not?"

"The couch didn't do anything to me."

"You are heartbroken that you never had the chance to say good-bye to your father. Would you like to write him a letter?"

"How would I mail it?"

He put the noodle down. "You must miss him dreadfully. Wouldn't you like to tell him that?"

"If I could tell him that, then I wouldn't be missing him."

The doctor drew a deep breath. "If you could say one thing to your father, what would it be?"

"What's it like to be dead?"

Clara saw this man a couple of more times; he tried to get her to draw with markers, punch and squash mounds of clay, talk to puppets, rip up old telephone books, go into a small, soundproof room and scream as loud as she could.

"She's not willing to do any of it," the doctor told Evil Lynn.

"That stubborn streak," Evil Lynn said.

The years passed, and Clara grew her limp brown hair out and kept her bangs long so you couldn't see her eyes. Her face rounded out like the moon, and she shot up practically overnight, between her tenth and eleventh birthdays, long skinny arms and legs like juice sticks. She began wearing denim overalls and flannel shirts in winter, and short overalls and T-shirts in summer, when Evil Lynn put her in day camps, which were like nonacademic versions of school. In both places Clara did what was required of her, nothing more or less.

Occasionally Kim called and sent messages, but Clara didn't answer her phone and ignored the texts and messages. What was the point? There was only room for one in the glass coffin. At school, when Kim tried talking about getting together, Clara said, "I'm really busy." With what, Kim asked her, and Clara just shrugged. Kim and her family moved to Belle Heights Tower, right across from Clara's apartment house. Clara never visited her. In the cafeteria, they didn't sit together; Clara told Kim she used this time to do crossword puzzles on her phone, planting herself at a corner table with a view of a brick wall.

Though sometimes Kim spoke to Clara as if nothing had gone wrong between them. When they had the same phys ed class, for instance, in seventh grade. Kim was one of Clara's spotters when Clara was on the trampoline. "C'mon, jump higher," Kim urged her. "Do a double turnaround seat drop! I've got your back." But Clara just did a regular seat drop.

Evil Lynn continued to take Clara to psychologists and therapists. "I believe there's something or someone out there who can help you," she explained. *Whatever works*, Evil Lynn made a point of saying again and again, whether they were trying talk therapy (which would have required Clara to talk), medication (which made her too sleepy), some new advance, an established treatment, or a combination; the list included anything that was reliable, proven, and safe.

Clara kept her word—or lack of it, ha-ha—when it came to

Evil Lynn, and only spoke to her when necessary. Clara's preferred method of communication was by Post-it. *I need this signed for school,* Clara would write on a Post-it stuck to a medical form. Or Evil Lynn might leave Clara a note on the kitchen table: *Going to the drugstore. Do you need soap?* Clara's answer: *No soap.* Which was one of her dad's expressions. It didn't mean he didn't want soap. It meant no deal, more or less.

Without discussing it, they worked out the household chores. Evil Lynn cleared the table and Clara did the dishes—always by hand; they had a dishwasher with powerful suction, but it shook so violently Clara thought it might explode at any moment. Clara also vacuumed and did the laundry, folding clothes in piles so neat they still looked like they were in the store. Evil Lynn did the grocery shopping and made breakfast and dinner. If Evil Lynn had to work late, Clara had frozen pizza. Clara kept her room clean, and Evil Lynn was not allowed to enter. If Clara got ready for school too slowly, Evil Lynn stood in the doorway and told her it was getting late. When that happened, Clara glared at her stepmother and made extra sure she hadn't set foot inside the room, not one inch, which, Clara was sure, would poison the atmosphere just as surely as Snow-white's stepmother had poisoned the apple.

CHAPTER 14

On Wednesday, October 17, Clara, fifteen and a half years old and a tenth grader at Belle Heights High, was about to dissect a virtual frog in bio lab.

Out of nowhere she heard a voice:

"Are you with us?"

Clara looked up to see Mr. Slocum hovering over her.

"I asked if you were with us, Miss Hartel." His bald head was turning purple. "You don't listen."

"I *am* listening." How could she explain that it only looked like she wasn't?

"You've been in my class for nearly six weeks. Do you think I haven't noticed you're in la-la land?"

"We're on it, Mr. Slocum," Selena Kearn jumped in, all freckles, dimples, and bouncy red curls. "I'm doing the setup, Astrid's taking notes, and Clara's doing the cutting."

"What?" Clara said.

They'd decided no such thing when the three of them had been assigned to this project. Of course Selena Kearn and Astrid Mills, who only hung out with other popular, good-looking, well-dressed kids, had made no secret of their displeasure at being partnered with Clara. They'd asked for somebody else, but Mr. Slocum never honored such requests.

Selena's sharp elbow jabbed Clara's ribs, right through the flannel shirt and denim overalls. "See, Clara's putting on the gloves right now. I'm allergic to latex, you know."

Mr. Slocum gazed at Clara as she put on a glove that was so tight it felt melted on. This took longer than it should have under his watchful eyes, and before she could get the other one on, he turned around and circled the room.

"Latex allergy, my ass," Astrid said, as Selena stuck out her lower lip.

Usually Clara didn't have a problem with schoolwork. It was like washing the dishes, something you did until it got done. But this was different, disturbing. The frog was about to be sliced open and exposed. *This isn't the way it's supposed to go,* Clara thought. *The outside is supposed to stay outside so the inside can stay inside.*

"I'll do the setup," Clara said. Selena hadn't done it yet. "I'll take notes." Astrid hadn't written anything yet, either. "But I don't want to cut."

"Grow up," Astrid said with an exaggerated sigh. She always acted as though all eyes were on her—and they usually were. "It's not even a real frog."

The computer spoke: "The purpose of this activity is to help you learn the anatomy of the frog by locating the major organs within the body cavity, which will give you a better understanding of all vertebrate animals, including humans."

"I hope you're paying attention, Clara," Astrid told her.

"Familiarize yourself with the materials," the computer said with some excitement—a recent audio upgrade to get kids engaged. Clara thought it had more emotion than some people did. "Look at the pan, the scalpel, forceps, scissors, pins, and the preserved frog. Notice the lower lid, the nonmovable upper lid, and the eyes, moistened by the nictitating membrane."

The eyes were a color Clara had never seen before. If it were in a big box of crayons, it could be called Cloudy Dead Blue.

"Notice the hearing organ of the frog, the tympanum," the computer said, increasingly upbeat. "It's the dark round circle behind the eyes, close to the jaw."

It was more than a dark round circle—it looked like a crater. Clara remembered how last year in geology, she'd learned about billion-year-old rocks, and how when meteors fell to earth, those rocks got thrown up to the surface, turned upside down, and thrust into the light when they should have stayed buried forever.

"I see you've got the gloves on," Mr. Slocum said, popping up again. "I don't see any work getting done."

"Clara's just thinking about the organs she's going to locate," Selena said.

Mr. Slocum left.

"You'd better get with it," Selena snapped. Her eyes were ferocious, but those freckles made her look like a little kid. "We all get graded the same, and if you mess this up . . ." She liked to leave things like that, unfinished and menacing.

"Place the frog in the pan on its back, belly up," the computer said gleefully. "Pin the frog through its hands and feet."

"Do it," Selena said. "He's watching us."

Actually Mr. Slocum had his back to them, but Clara picked up a virtual pin. She touched the frog's back leg with the sharp point. The skin felt lumpy, squishy, and resistant. It popped, and the needle slid right through the flesh to the pan.

"Finally," Astrid breathed out. She had perfect, pouty lips. Selena said she wanted to get her own lips puffed, to look like Astrid's. Clara had seen a video about that.

"What're you gonna be for Halloween?" Selena asked Astrid.

"A spider."

"I'm gonna be the girl singer in the Cadaver Dogs."

Clara didn't know the music of the Cadaver Dogs, or the cutest actors in Hollywood, or the latest episode of the shows everybody else was watching. These things weren't on her radar. She didn't care about Halloween, either, or about her birthday in April, or the seven-year anniversary of her dad's death in just a few weeks—November something. She could never remember the exact date. At some point in the early part of November, Evil Lynn always lit a candle.

"This one could be a ghost," Astrid said, referring to Clara. "It's like she's haunting the place."

"She wouldn't even need a costume." Selena laughed.

Astrid and Selena never censored their snarky comments in front of Clara, whether about Clara herself or about other kids, knowing Clara would never repeat them to another kid or report them to a teacher, or even say anything to indicate she'd been listening. They were particularly cruel about Kim, making fun of her mismatched clothes and the fact that she couldn't afford to eat lunch out. Astrid's latest was "Kim Garcia should have her memory entirely wiped and start from scratch. Anything would be an improvement." Occasionally it occurred to Clara to stick up for her old friend, but she never did.

"Ow, I shouldn't laugh, these things are killing me," Selena said. She had the latest thing in orthodontics, Bracelesses, tiny adjustable magnets embedded in your teeth. They cost a fortune, but the video Clara had seen about them was right, they were invisible. "Brace yourself!" the announcer intoned. "You won't believe your eyes—or your smile." Whenever Clara started watching videos like these, she couldn't stop. By swiping left she could cut them off after three seconds, but she often tapped on them and went to the advertiser's channel to watch the whole thing, however long it was. Of course the more she watched, the more advertisers targeted her. There was probably a setting on her phone to disable these videos altogether, but why do that? They were so clever, so penetrating, the way they could isolate one specific thing that was imperfect, whether you knew about it or not, and then solve it like magic. Though she'd seen a couple about memory alteration, which frankly sounded sort of crazy.

"Stop complaining," Astrid said to Selena.

"But they *hurt*. How can something you can't even see hurt so much?"

"I have a paper cut," Astrid said. "You can't see it, but it hurts like hell. Do you hear me whining?"

"This morning I bit the inside of my cheek," Clara said without thinking.

Selena and Astrid exchanged a look and then burst out laughing.

"Ow," Selena said.

"It's time for the first incision," the computer chirped in.

"Well, go on," Selena said. "What are you waiting for?"

Selena had done nothing so far. Astrid had only turned on the computer. Clara looked at the pinned-down frog and its white belly with faint beige spots. You could practically see through that belly to the dark organs and blue veins.

"Use the scalpel to cut along the center, or midline, of the frog," the computer said, "bisecting it equally."

Clara lifted the virtual scalpel and held it in midair.

"Use the scalpel to cut along the center, or midline, of the frog, bisecting it equally," the computer said in a more scolding tone. Apparently it didn't like to repeat itself.

"Come on already," Selena snapped. "Bio ends in ten minutes. Do you want to get marked down?"

Clara held the scalpel to the frog's throat and moved the scalpel down its belly.

"In a *straight* line," Selena said.

Clara's cut slanted wildly.

"Continue to cut, now with scissors," the computer said, regaining its composure. "Be careful not to cut too deeply."

That wasn't the problem. Clara wasn't cutting deeply enough.

"Look," Selena said. "Nick and Dylan have already found the heart and liver."

They weren't the only ones. All around the room, other computers were way ahead, cheerfully instructing:

"Separate the skin and muscle; notice the abdominal region...."

"Pin the muscle flaps to allow easy access to the internal organs...."

"Lift the liver gently to observe the lungs...."

"Notice the heart, the red potato with tubes on top. It resembles a human heart...."

While their computer said, sourly, "Continue to cut, now with scissors. Be careful not to cut too deeply." Abruptly it beeped loudly and said, "Instructions have been repeated repeatedly. Do you need me to alert the teacher?"

"You're hopeless," Astrid said.

Mr. Slocum was suddenly there again.

"Clara won't do what she agreed to do," Selena told him. "Meanwhile Astrid and I are doing all the work, and we have to share a grade with her!"

"Well?" Mr. Slocum said to Clara. "Explain yourself."

Clara tried. "The heart is on the inside, the skin on the

outside. So it's already the way it's supposed to be. Don't you see? The heart, the potato heart, looks like a real heart—and we shouldn't see that."

Mr. Slocum looked at her for several long moments. Finally he said, loud enough for the entire class to hear, "Miss Hartel, report to Ms. Pratt."

Not to Mr. Silver, the principal, but to Ms. Pratt, the school psychologist. Selena and Astrid exchanged a look of satisfaction. Clara peeled off her gloves. Her fingers were as wrinkled as if she'd taken a long bath. She grabbed her backpack.

"Lesson ended due to inactivity," the computer said, and then shut off.

"Oh no!" Selena wailed to Mr. Slocum. "Will this affect our grade?"

"How can it not?" Mr. Slocum said.

"That's seriously not fair!" Selena stomped her foot.

"Life isn't fair," Mr. Slocum said.

Neither is death, it occurred to Clara. *And that doesn't leave much else.*

CHAPTER 15

Clara waited on a wooden bench next to Ms. Pratt's office. The pale October sky was turning orange, and she could see a tattered net on the basketball court outside. It was quiet except for muffled voices behind Ms. Pratt's door.

The door opened—and out came Kim Garcia. She had on a ruffled orange shirt and sweatpants. "What happened?" she said to Clara with a worried look.

"It's nothing." Clara had long fingers, and she tangled them like vines. "Just a misunderstanding."

"Well, I'm here for something completely stupid. I was in the library when Nick Winter, that idiot, knocked over a lamp, because he and Dylan Beck were goofing around, shoving each other. The librarian collected everybody's names in case she needed to talk to us later—about the 'incident'—and I got mad because, you know, I had nothing to do with it, so I signed a fake name. Which made them think I was losing it."

Clara didn't mean to, but she couldn't help asking, "What name did you use?"

"Alison Wanda Landa. It's actually a girl in my building. Her dad's a dentist, Dr. Landa, and he named his daughter Alison Wanda."

There, Kim was doing it again, acting as if nothing had gone wrong between them. Usually Clara would just not respond; sometimes she would cut the conversation short, in order to remind Kim they weren't close anymore.

But now, for just a second, Clara felt how it used to be with her and Kim, as if no time had passed, and the entire last seven years hadn't happened yet. "That's the dumbest name I ever heard," she said with some energy.

"I know, right?"

The door opened. "You may come in now," said a woman.

It wasn't Ms. Pratt.

The woman looked as young as a teenager herself, in a corduroy dirndl and feathery ash-blond hair with two tiny floating butterfly barrettes clipped to her head. That was last year's big thing. Selena had worn them all through ninth grade and wouldn't be caught dead in them now.

"You're not Ms. Pratt." Clara jutted her chin at the door, which clearly said MS. PRATT.

"Ms Pratt had a family emergency. I am Ms. Gruskin." She smiled, displaying a butterfly tattoo on her front tooth. She smelled like strawberries. "What is your name?"

Clara told her.

"Do you have an appointment?"

"I was sent."

"Won't you come in and have a seat?"

Clara knew this office—she'd been here a few times in ninth grade and once already in tenth. Evil Lynn had insisted that Clara make appointments with the psychologist in middle school and now in high school, too. Ms. Pratt was nice enough, but of course Clara had nothing to say to her.

She sat on the couch across from Ms. Gruskin at the desk and stared at tall flowers trapped in a vase filled with stones and water. The indentation in the couch fit perfectly, as if Kim, her friend from long ago, had made a point of breaking it in for her.

"Who sent you here?"

"Mr. Slocum."

"And he teaches—?"

"Bio."

"Why did he send you?"

"I couldn't cut into a virtual frog."

Ms. Gruskin's butterflies sagged. "Help me to understand, Clara. You know that all dissections are virtual these days. I can see being opposed to the killing of live animals—in the old days kids held chloroform over the mouths of frogs until they were dead, if you can imagine that. But these frogs were never alive, so what's the problem?"

Clara tangled her fingers again. Music teachers often said it was a shame she didn't want to play piano. She had the perfect hands for it.

"Perhaps if I knew something about you, Clara, I'd understand this better. When you're not in school, what do you do? For fun."

"Crossword puzzles."

"That is fun! I can do the *New York Times* Monday and Tuesday puzzles, but once it gets to Wednesday, no thank you! Do you do sports? You're so tall. I always wished I were taller! Do you play basketball?"

Clara was almost six feet. Basketball coaches used to pursue her, and she had to tell them she wasn't interested. Piano, basketball—maybe her body was suited to those things, but Clara wasn't.

"What about clubs? The school musical? I hear it's *Into the Woods* this year. I love that show. Do you know the song that says 'Children will listen'?"

"Try telling that to Mr. Slocum," Clara said under her breath.

Ms. Gruskin cocked her head, but Clara had nothing to add.

"Tell me about your friends, Clara. In the cafeteria, do you eat at a big crowded table with lots of kids, or with only one special friend?"

"I eat by myself." She would do a crossword puzzle and eat a poppy-seed bagel with cream cheese and three chocolate chip cookies that came in a pack. The bushy-haired kid at the scanner sometimes said things like "Why don't you surprise me sometime, with oatmeal-raisin cookies instead? Astound me with a sesame-seed bagel! I hope my heart can take it." Clara always ignored him.

"Are you bullied? It's a special interest of mine. I'm writing a book about it."

Selena and Astrid could qualify as bullies, but even anonymously, Clara didn't want anyone writing about her in a book.

"Do you get along with your parents?"

"My parents are dead."

"Oh! I didn't know. . . . Do you live with a guardian?"

"I wouldn't call her that."

"You are no stranger to death, then. Not to imply that you and death are *friends*, necessarily. That's another interest of mine, a death in the family. I'm writing a book for children called *When Some Bunny Dies*. Young children must hear the truth, no sugar-coating. You should never say, about the deceased parent, 'She's sleeping,' or the child will think Mommy is sure to wake up. You should never say, 'We lost him.' Then the child might go searching for Daddy. In my book, Mama Bunny tells it to Baby Bunny straight out—'Papa Bunny dropped dead.' Now I have to call your—what did you say she was?"

"Stepmother." Clara gave her the number.

Ms. Gruskin made the call. She explained in a whisper, but loud enough for Clara to hear, why Clara had been sent to her. Then she hung up and turned around. "She didn't sound surprised."

That didn't surprise Clara.

Ms. Gruskin frowned. "You'll have to check in with me next

week, or with Ms. Pratt if she's back by then. So I guess that's it, unless you wish to discuss the frog?"

Clara shook her head.

"Anything else you'd like to share?"

"Should I wait in the hall?"

"Yes." Ms. Gruskin breathed out, sounding relieved.

Clara went back to the bench. School had just ended and Nick Winter was outside, throwing a basketball. He was tall and wore a team tank top, which left his arms exposed so he could flex them every time he took a shot. A few girls hovered, admiring him. Orange light from outside settled over Clara as she waited for her stepmother.

CHAPTER 16

Evil Lynn showed up looking marvelously put together, as always, not a single hair out of place even when the wind blew. She was curvy and athletic and wore clothes effortlessly, as if they had been designed for her, blouses and pants that on anybody else might look okay, nothing special.

As they walked, the sky, now smeared with dark orange, gray, salmon pink, and purple, caused people all around them to stop and point and admire. Clara, though, looked straight ahead and never slowed; such things were lost on her—nothing to write home about, as her dad used to say. Walking along Belle Heights Drive, she saw peeling paint on some of the storefronts and a mannequin in a thrift-shop window that was missing an arm. At Fully Baked, the window, filled with miniature glazed cupcakes, had a sign that had been there forever, promising "all the colors of the rainbow." But that, as Clara made a point of noticing, didn't include Cloudy Dead Blue. Off Belle Heights

Drive, they walked along curvy, hilly streets where the rows of houses had straggly lawns out front. It wasn't dark yet, but streetlights came on and cast a bluish glow.

"Acupuncture," Evil Lynn said suddenly. "You've never tried it."

Clara pictured herself on a dissecting tray. "Is that where they stick you full of pins?"

"You don't feel it."

Clara found that highly unlikely.

"Don't forget—we already have an appointment tomorrow at Neuro Plus, a biofeedback place. It's in the mall in Spruce Hills, but don't let that fool you. It's highly reputable. So don't make any plans after school."

As if Clara ever had plans.

Evil Lynn was persistent, you had to give her that, despite failure after failure. In her bedroom she had a whole bookshelf full of child-development books. Sometimes Clara flipped through them when Evil Lynn wasn't home, and saw things highlighted in yellow: *Some psychiatrists believe that true mourning is not possible until adolescence; only then can the older child process the younger child's pain.* Evil Lynn had underlined that as well with a thick black marker, and added: *???*

Phrases Clara didn't understand leaped out at her: *Integrate the traumatic event of the death within the psychic structure of the bereaved . . . move beyond shock and numbness to despair and sorrow, and finally to remembering and mastering the events with an eye toward the reorientation and equilibrium of the self and object.*

Just last month Evil Lynn had researched Chinese herbs and brought home bags of yellow and brown powders. She looked positively witchy, sifting powders together and placing the mixture in clear capsules that had no effect on Clara.

Clara felt her phone buzz.

But her phone *never* buzzed anymore.

She opened her phone and saw Selena's ID pic jump out at her, big smile, freckles, dimples. Her message, however, had flames shooting from the words:

> Mr. S got computer back on but Astrid had to rush
> & pierced the heart & we all got D-minus on the frog
> thanx to you meaning no thanx.

All at once Clara bumped into someone. It was entirely Clara's fault—she'd been staring at her flaming phone. She glanced up and saw a girl about her age. She wore a jean jacket and her lipstick was dramatically red. She had short dark hair just above her chin; on one side her hair was behind her ear, and on the other it was in front. She held a leash, which led to a small dog in a sweater.

Clara ought to apologize.

But the girl gave her a big, warm, open, completely spontaneous smile and said, "Oops."

In that moment Clara felt an intense surge from her innermost core to the outermost reaches of her being:

Change places with me.

One of the therapists Clara had been taken to had told her that every thought and emotion reached out to every cell in the body. It hadn't made sense until now. With everything in her and more, Clara wanted to be this girl in the jean jacket, think her thoughts, live her life—which Clara could already imagine with perfect clarity. This girl was on her way to meet her friends, because of course this girl had lots of friends, and they'd all listen to music or go to a movie, it wouldn't matter what, because just being together would be wonderful by itself. And they'd send messages to one another because they had something funny to say, not messages burning with leaping flames. And time would just zip by, not drag from one moment to the next. This girl was kind and had a big heart; she loved animals, clearly—she'd put a sweater on her dog—and she reached out to those in need, people who seemed lonely, and everyone remarked on it, what a good soul she was. Her parents were so proud and astounded by how lucky they were, having such a daughter.

If only, Clara thought, *I could change places with her. Not that she'd ever want to....*

Although—some ads for memory manipulation and the new techniques available had popped up on her phone. She'd never checked out the long versions. If Clara could somehow slide this girl's memories into her head, replacing her own, that would be just as good, right?

Or, no—it sounded too crazy.

Clara, who wouldn't stop for sunsets, turned to watch the

girl walk away. There was a large embroidered rose on the back of the jean jacket. Clara had never seen anything like it: layers of gorgeous red petals, maybe a little uneven; she imagined the girl's mother hand sewing it. *Here, try it on,* she could hear the girl's mother say. *Now go to the mirror and turn around.*

Why should I—?

Look over your shoulder.

Oh . . .

Do you like it?

I love it!

CHAPTER 17

Clara's block, with its complex of two-family redbrick houses arranged in a long line of two-story buildings, felt crowded and claustrophobic to her, with pairs of families on top of one another and stuck to other pairs on either side, all in the long shadow of the monstrous Belle Heights Tower.

Upstairs from Clara and Evil Lynn lived an old lady who had always had two enormous dogs. At night Clara could hear their toenails clicking on the floor overhead. Didn't the old lady have carpeting?

As it happened, the old lady was coming downstairs just as Clara and Evil Lynn reached their front door, those huge dogs panting heavily and pulling at their leashes. One of them barked, shrill and hollow; it echoed in the stairway.

"Do you see that sunset? Isn't it breathtaking?" The old lady always tried to engage Clara in conversation, but Clara never, ever engaged back.

Evil Lynn took a moment to agree that the sunset was lovely.

"Oh, my dear, you look terrified," the old lady said.

"I'm fine," Clara said, even as she felt her breath catch in her throat. Those dogs could lunge at you, it suddenly occurred to her, not just want to lick your hand. How would you know, until it was too late?

"But my dear, they wouldn't hurt a soul!"

Clara went straight to her room, closed the door, and waited for her heart to stop thudding. She grabbed the old elephant, the stiff, bald toy that had belonged to her mom, and held on for dear life.

That night Clara did the dishes; hot soapy water bubbled up between her long fingers. Usually she wore dishwashing gloves, but after that bio lab she would never wear them again.

Evil Lynn, in a striped red-and-black kimono, sat watching TV in the living room on the couch she had reupholstered herself. Clara had liked the old, faded, wheat-colored fabric, despite several large holes shredded around the edges; Kim used to say it looked like a stray cat had snuck in during the night. Now the couch had a dark floral pattern Clara had never warmed up to. Over the years Evil Lynn had done other things to the place that seemed, well, out of place. A piece of yellow silk draped over the back of her dad's favorite blue chair was an obvious mistake, because it kept sliding down. A huge rug from a flea market, disgusting. Who knew anything about the people who'd owned it before? And hanging up a patchwork quilt—why would anyone put a blanket on the wall? Blankets belonged on beds.

On-screen Clara saw a young woman who looked sad and scared and lost.

"What's wrong with her?" Clara blurted out.

Evil Lynn turned, surprised to see Clara standing behind her, even more surprised that Clara was speaking to her. She cleared her throat. "She thinks her husband is still in love with his first wife. This girl is rather plain and awkward, and terribly shy, and the first wife was sophisticated and gorgeous."

Clara stared at the actress. She was actually very pretty, with soft, swept-back brown hair and beautiful dark eyes, but she looked so deeply unhappy, even as she insisted to her husband, "We're happy, aren't we? Terribly happy?"

Clara's dad had met Evil Lynn at a bus stop. They'd both been waiting for a long time before someone showed up and told them the bus stop had been moved to a different street because a water main had burst. Together Clara's dad and Evil Lynn had walked to the temporary bus stop, taken the bus, begun dating, and were married only a few months later. At which point he said this was partly for Clara's sake! "I didn't want to introduce you to a string of women," he'd said, smiling gently. "I wanted something everlasting."

There was a photo in the living room of Clara's real mother, her hair a mass of dark-brown curls, head tilted, crinkles at the corners of her eyes, laughing. She hadn't been *everlasting*—she'd had thyroid cancer, one of the cancers with an incredibly high survival rate except for the few who were unlucky. Clara used to touch her throat, where the thyroid is, and hum, trying to feel this thing that had killed her mother. As for the thing that had killed her dad, all she had to do was hold her hand over her heart. But she didn't do it.

"Plus," her dad had said about her stepmother, "I saw something amazing in her right away. There's a quality there—very unusual."

Clara had never seen it, not a glimmer. Not then, not now.

"What's her name?" Clara asked about the woman on-screen.

Evil Lynn kept her eyes on the TV and spoke. "She doesn't have a name."

"That's not possible."

"The movie is called *Rebecca*—"

Clara folded her arms. "Then her name is Rebecca."

"Rebecca was the first wife, who died."

"But everybody has a name!" Clara had moved closer to Evil Lynn, without thinking, and caught the smell of lavender.

"She has a name," Evil Lynn said. "We just never learn what it is. Maybe because she lives in the shadow of a ghost, the ghost of Rebecca. The girl thinks Rebecca must've been the perfect wife, but it turns out Rebecca was vindictive and cruel and used people dreadfully, and the husband never loved her. In fact, it turns out he ended up killing Rebecca. In the movie it's an accident. In the book it's definitely murder. So you see, not everyone is what they seem. Sometimes you think somebody's wonderful but she's not, and the opposite can be true, too—"

"Does the new wife have a name in the book?" Clara didn't care about any of the rest of it.

"No, she narrates and we never learn it there, either."

But a name was—well, important. It gave you a place on earth that was yours alone. Clara stood there in the living room, watching and waiting and longing for someone to call this woman by her name, but no one ever did. There would have been so many just-right names for her—Rose, for instance, which was so simple but contained so much, beauty plus a thorn to protect her.

CHAPTER 18

There was a Post-it on the kitchen table the next morning: *Don't forget—appt. today.*

Clara shook her head. When would Evil Lynn give up?

At lunch, the kid at the scanner remarked to her, "You used to be a friend of Kim's," and Clara heard herself say, "I *am* a friend of Kim's," and then caught sight of Kim, who had on a Mets jersey and turquoise harem pants, no doubt from Second Nature because no regular store had carried them in years. The old tug of their friendship pulled at her, the dumb things they'd done; in kindergarten they'd hidden in a storage closet during a fire drill, laughing their heads off. Their teacher got so mad when they were found, and got so much madder when Clara kept saying, "But it wasn't a *real* fire." Before she knew it she was putting her tray down and sitting opposite Kim and asking, "Okay if I sit with you?"

"Well, sure," Kim said right away, flipping her braid behind her.

What was happening here? Last night, Clara had actually shed tears, just a few, at an old movie simply because a woman looked so alone and had no name. Clara *never* cried. Yesterday afternoon, she'd practically broken out in hives over a couple of dogs owned by an old lady she had, without effort, been able to ignore for years. Now she had joined Kim for lunch. She had no idea what to say.

Kim didn't seem to mind; she shrugged her shoulders. "So . . . you want to do a crossword puzzle?"

What a great idea. Clara pulled out her phone and held it between them. A video for Bracelesses popped up, but she swiped it away.

"I've never really done one before," Kim said.

Clara showed her how you started with the words moving across, or horizontally. The clue for one across: six-letter word for *ache*.

"Pain," Clara said. "Wait, that's only four letters. Anguish— that's seven, too many, distress, also seven, what about agony? Oh, that's five."

"Desire," Kim said.

Clara said the easy way to check if your word was correct was to take a quick look at an intersecting word—say, one down. The clue: *Personal journal* (five letters). That had to be *diary*, and the *d* confirmed that the first letter of one across was also *d*. Kim had gotten it right. Clara had been on the wrong track.

The puzzle was a tricky one—they got harder as the week went along—but it turned out Kim was a natural, as Clara told her while eating her poppy-seed bagel and chocolate chip cookies. Kim had something she'd brought from home, an avocado-and-turkey spiral. Together they finished the puzzle in less than fifteen minutes, faster than Clara had ever done a Thursday puzzle.

"Hey, I've been looking around for someone," Kim said. "I wasn't going to ask you, because, you know . . ." She paused. "But you'd be perfect, Clara. You have the best face."

What was that?

"I want to put stage makeup on you—I need the practice, and this would really help. A girl in the cast got me to sign up to do the play this year, *Into the Woods*, and I want them all to look just right. Your face is so wide open, so inviting. I look at you and I see—so many possibilities. I could turn you into anything. With makeup, I mean. Please say yes."

Clara thought about it—and found she had absolutely no thoughts about it whatsoever. "Okay."

"Yay!" Kim actually clapped. "Can you come over today, after school?"

"Tomorrow," Clara said quickly. "Today I have . . . plans."

Hydro-buses were always way too crowded in Belle Heights, and it also took an extra-long time for passengers to get on and off. The ladder in the center slowed everything down, so most people bunched up toward the ramp at the front. That way you boarded the bus faster, but usually there were no seats to be had. Clara and Evil Lynn ended up standing up the whole way, people jostling them on either side, and there was a vague smell of something sour. The bus kept stalling, which upped the annoyance factor, all the way to Spruce Hills, which, contrary to its name, didn't have a single hill (or any spruce trees, for that matter).

Inside the mall, Evil Lynn took her to Neuro Plus, which was between a tattoo parlor and a Bracelesses store. Selena probably came here for adjustments. Clara was grateful to see no sign of her.

Once inside, Clara sat in a waiting area that was really a long hall. She had Evil Lynn on one side and two women deep in conversation on the other. At one point the first one said, "Is that your new coat?"

"It's *one* of my new coats," said the other.

After a time a man stood before them. He had a thick mustache the color and texture of straw. "I am Dr. Stone," he said.

Clara got up.

Dr. Stone looked somewhat alarmed. Sometimes her height threw people off.

"She's fifteen," Evil Lynn remarked.

"Of course. We see many children. Won't you follow me?" Dr. Stone signaled for Evil Lynn to stay where she was, something she was accustomed to doing when it came to waiting areas. She had come prepared; a thick book was in her lap.

Dr. Stone led Clara to a tiny room; it barely held his desk and chair, and a chair for her. But he spoke expansively: "We at Neuro Plus begin with biofeedback, a form of therapy that enables you to monitor your brain-wave activity." He leaned back in his chair, hitting the wall. "I do that every time!" he said with a laugh.

Clara appreciated that he'd admitted it, didn't try to cover it up. A few photos sat on his desk. Good-looking African American wife, really good-looking kids. In one of the pictures he had them in his arms like he couldn't get enough of them.

"Think of what happens to the body that is about to have an anxiety attack. The breathing becomes rapid. The blood pressure rises. The heart rate increases. The palms sweat. There is muscle tension in the head, neck, and back. Finally the body experiences a full-blown anxiety attack. Not a pretty picture, is it? But with the help of biofeedback, the body will be able to recognize and even anticipate these symptoms. The body will learn to relax and prevent the attack before it has a chance to happen." He opened his arms. "It's quite a wonderful thing."

"But not for me," Clara said. "I don't have anxiety attacks."

"Your stepmother believes you have something like an 'adjustment disorder,'" Dr. Stone said, softening his voice, "which can be short-lived. In your case, not. It's a kind of anxiety attack with its own set of brain signals. You could learn which signals are sending you the wrong messages and make the appropriate modifications."

Adjustment disorder. So, it had a name.

"Your case requires more than biofeedback, however. Talk therapy, at the very least—conversations. It's not something that happens overnight; it does take time: months, sometimes even years. But there's steady progress along the way." He was speaking even more quietly now, as if he didn't want anyone else to hear. But no one else was in the room. "You see, Clara, you are grieving as a child."

"I'm not a child," Clara said sharply.

"In life you are fifteen, but in your grief you are eight."

This made no sense. She was fifteen, not eight, and she didn't want to listen to brain messages and she certainly didn't want to talk. If she wanted to do anything at all, it was to change places with the girl in the jean jacket. How could biofeedback help her with that?

"Are you all right?" Dr. Stone asked her. "You look a little shaky."

"I'm fine," Clara said.

"Why don't you give it a try?" Dr. Stone said. "It's remarkably easy—I hook you up to a machine, and your bodily reactions can be observed in real time on a screen. Seeing your physiological responses can begin the process of controlling them, which leads to reactive mastery, as we call it."

Clara shook her head.

"It's perfectly safe, a clinically proven method that's been around for decades—unlike one of these fly-by-night, quick-fix neurological outfits with their memory additions and subtractions. It's why Neuro Plus appealed to your stepmother so much."

"Then let her do it."

"This can help you," Dr. Stone said—and sounded genuinely concerned, Clara noticed. "It's already helped many others. But you must be invested. Positive results only come when a patient is invested."

Dr. Stone told Evil Lynn he was sorry he couldn't refund her money, but he could arrange for credit should Clara ever change her mind.

Clara was relieved to leave, and even more so that Selena wasn't anywhere to be seen.

CHAPTER 19

Friday afternoon was dark and blustery cold. Clara shivered as she and Kim walked to Belle Heights Tower, and her teeth were still chattering in the elevator that took them up to the fourteenth floor. "I'm sorry," Kim said. "I should have brought you a coat."

Clara remembered that Kim never got cold, at least not until it was really freezing, and when they were kids had always brought a heavy jacket to school, just in case Clara wanted to borrow it. There was something so familiar about being with Kim, even if Clara didn't really know what she was doing here.

Kim pointed out that the floor numbers went directly from twelve to fourteen. "It's really the thirteenth floor," she said. "Who are they kidding?"

Ha, Kim *would* live on a floor that didn't actually exist.

Once inside Kim's apartment, Clara headed for the window and looked down at her own two-story apartment house, seeing its flat gray roof and redbrick chimney for the first time.

"It's always amazed me that you live so close," Kim said. "You could've popped over anytime."

But to Clara it felt like an infinite distance, one that also stretched way back in time, as if she was peering out at something in the long-ago past.

Clara looked around the living room and recognized some of the furniture that had followed Kim here from her old place near Belle Heights Bay, a couple of recliners, an old love seat with curvy legs that ended in lion's feet, a big coffee table with a glass top, and lots of books.

"Let's work in the bathroom; I need the sink," Kim said. "I'm really glad you're here, Clara. You and that face of yours." They went to the bathroom. "You mind washing up?"

"You know I don't have to wash any makeup off."

"I like to work on a clean slate."

Clara used the soap in the soap dish—it was the same kind Evil Lynn used, lavender, sticky sweet. When Clara was finished, Kim motioned for her to sit on top of the closed toilet seat, which had a fuzzy blue cover that matched the blue towels.

"Okay, now for the 'before' pictures. This'll help me see what I've done right and any stuff that's not right. You don't have to smile if you don't want to." Kim checked the photos and said, "Want to see?"

Clara shook her head.

Kim rummaged through a tote bag with several bottles, tubes, pencils, brushes, powders, and pastes before opening a small jar. "This stuff ate up nearly all my babysitting money," she said, smearing some creamy goo on Clara's face. "Last weekend I babysat this kid Mark, who lives down on the third floor. Do you know he asked me for cotton balls before he went to bed? And I gave him some. I mean, cotton balls, what's the big deal? When his mother got home, she said, you didn't give him cotton balls, did you, and I said, well, yeah, and she freaked. She said, I told you not to—Mark *eats* cotton balls! I said, you never told me, I would've remembered something weird like that, and she said, it's not weird and I did tell you. I mean, if my kid did that, I'd put it on a sign on his bedroom door—Don't Give This Kid Cotton Balls. Turns out Mark hadn't eaten any, he just had them clumped in his fist, but the mom was so mad she didn't want to pay me. And I'd been there six hours! Luckily, the dad slipped me some money." Kim dusted Clara's face with something that felt like snow without the cold. "So, let me tell you about yourself."

"There's nothing to say, Kim."

"No, I mean, your character, the one I'm inventing for you. Makeup is all about make up, get it? The outside is supposed to show the inside."

Kim had it so exactly wrong. The outside was meant to protect and hide and deny the very existence of the inside, as she'd tried to explain to Mr. Slocum, whose only response had been to send her to the school psychologist.

"Let's see. You're an old lady. Everything has passed you by. Friendship and love and success and happiness. Your whole life you waited for a bus, but it didn't stop for you. Now give me a big smile."

And what kind of smile would there be after a life with no friendship or love or success or happiness? She smiled hesitantly.

"Bigger. Eyebrows way up. That's it. The purpose of a smile is to show where your eye wrinkles will be. I won't do every one, or you'd look like a road map." Kim filled in half a dozen feathery lines radiating out from the corners of the eyes. "Now make a mad face. Good! That way I can see your forehead wrinkles." She used a gray-brown pencil, heavy in the middle of the forehead and fading at the ends. She colored in a few circles on the temples—these were age spots. Then she added dark smoky powder on the sides of the nose and the hollows of the eye sockets. "Your skin is incredible; it shows everything." When Kim reached Clara's neck, Clara tensed.

"It tickles," she said.

"I'll do it fast. I have to do all your exposed skin. I could put a scarf on you, but that would be cheating. If you were really onstage, I'd do your hands, too, lots of showy veins and more age spots."

Clara clenched her teeth. It was really ticklish. "How do you even know how to do this?"

"YouTube. There are tons of tutorials; I've seen every one. Couple of years ago, I saw a play where a man had this weird skin condition that turned him into a lizard. I've been fascinated by stage makeup ever since." Finally, Kim finished her neck. "Now, it's time for your hair. An old lady like you can't have light-brown hair."

"You never said anything about dyeing my hair!" This was something Clara would never do. She trimmed her own hair with a few snips every six months or so, keeping her bangs just long enough so you couldn't see her eyes.

"Don't worry; this stuff will wash right out." Kim spread some thick paste on an old toothbrush. "It looks yellow out of the tube, but winds up looking gray in your hair." She pushed Clara's hair back off her forehead, flattening it, so she could get at the roots and work her way to the ends. It dried almost instantly and felt like cement.

"I'd like to make your character's life worse, if that's okay with you."

"In for a penny, in for a pound." One of those things Clara's dad used to say. Basically, it meant go ahead.

"Let's say you got beaten for years. So you've got old scars and new bruises. Just to add insult to injury. Or is it injury to insult?" Kim applied a much darker shadow next to the nose and three colors to the curve under the right eye—gray-violet, slate gray, maroon red. "A little gloss, too—a shiner should always have some shine. Now for some scar liquid."

The skin near the right side of Clara's mouth pinched and tightened, like she was permanently sneering. That side of her nose felt pulled in the wrong direction.

Kim stepped back and picked up her phone again. "Time

for the 'after' pictures," she said, clicking away. She scrolled through the photos. "Hey, looks fantastic—even better than I'd hoped! Nothing to touch up. Want to take a good look at yourself?"

There was a mirror over the sink.

Clara stood and looked at her reflection. She saw an old, old woman, her face overtaken by wrinkles and age spots, with a broken nose, a black eye, and the remnants of a wound near her lower lip.

The outside, Clara realized, no longer turned you away from the inside. It was exposing it, holding it up to the light, demanding that it be seen.

"So, what do you think?" Kim asked cheerfully.

That's me; that's what I am, Clara thought. *The bus didn't stop, and the whole rest of my life will be spent catching up to the image in the mirror until the outside matches the inside. And then I'll die, simple as that.*

"Clara, I wish you'd say something." Kim gave her shoulder a gentle nudge. "Do you like it?"

"It's exactly right," Clara said. "Dead-on accurate."

Kim let out a little laugh. "I might do something like this for the witch in *Into the Woods*. But she's supposed to be young and beautiful at the end—maybe it would be too hard to get all this stuff off between acts?"

"It would be impossible," Clara said with certainty.

"You're probably right." Kim caught her breath. "Oh, Clara."

"What?"

"You—you're trembling."

"I'm not."

"Look at your hands."

Clara gazed at her hands, surprised they were still young looking.

"Here, why don't you wash up?" Kim handed her some wet wipes, the type for baby bottoms. "You may have to shampoo twice to get the gray out."

Forcefully, Clara used the wipes, every last one. "You have any more?"

"I think you got it all off."

"I need a picture for my phone."

"From before or after?"

"After." The "before" pictures were meaningless.

Clara got out her phone, received the photo, and slotted it in as her ID pic.

"So," Kim began, "do you maybe want to stay for dinner? My mom—"

"I have to go," Clara said without looking at Kim.

Kim bit her lower lip. "Clara, what's wrong? I don't know what happened—c'mon, let's just go to my room and—"

"No, I really, really have to go." It was too late already. It was over. Why couldn't Kim see what was plain as day?

At home Clara rushed to the shower. She washed her hair three separate times and practically scrubbed herself raw, getting rid of the gray, any last traces of makeup, and that smell of Kim's lavender soap. And she was trying with all her might, as if it were even possible, to wash out the inside.

No soap.

CHAPTER 20

It was late that same Friday. Clara sat in the big blue armchair in the living room, legs tucked beneath her. She had her phone open and was looking at the ID pic Kim had taken. How long had she been doing this? She had no idea.

Evil Lynn swept into the room. She wore a plain off-white kimono. Earlier, Clara had seen her gazing in the mirror at her own glowing, youthful appearance, head to foot, the fairest in the land, scrutinizing every inch of herself as if she didn't want to miss out on any of it. Such a different experience from Clara's.

"I spoke to a child-development specialist earlier," she said.

"I'm not a child." If only Evil Lynn knew how old she really was.

"She works with teenagers, too. I wish—I wish I knew what to do, Clara. I'm at the point—"

"There's nothing to be done." Clara had seen her future. She was looking at it that very minute.

"What is it, Clara, why are you shouting?"

Was she? She could practically hear the echo of her words in the air. *There's nothing to be done.*

"What are you looking at?" Evil Lynn came closer, bringing with her the cloying scent of lavender, so sticky sweet.

Clara handed over her phone.

"Who is that poor woman? Where did you see her?"

"Don't you recognize her?"

"I hope you called the police."

"Look closer," Clara urged her.

Evil Lynn stared at the picture, and at Clara, then back at the picture and back once more at Clara. "I don't understand."

Clara grabbed her phone back.

At three a.m. Clara woke from a nightmare.

Clara hardly ever dreamed, or at least hardly ever remembered dreaming, maybe because she slept so fitfully. But this one had followed her into waking and still surrounded and clung to her.

In the dream she was dressed as she was now, in a granny nightgown. There was an explosion. Clara wasn't sure how she knew this, because there'd been no bright light or booming sound. She was standing at her bedroom window, looking out at Belle Heights Tower. It was on fire. Clara saw a flickering light in the window. And someone there. Was it Kim? In the dream, Clara grew desperate.

Get out of there! Clara wanted to yell at the top of her voice.

Now! But whoever it was only stared back.

Clara looked more closely. It wasn't Kim—but an old, old woman. What Clara was seeing was a reflection. Belle Heights Tower wasn't on fire. Clara was in the burning building. The flames were at her back and coming closer.

Clara had sat up then, fully awake, in the circle of light from the lamp near her bed.

It was a dream, just a dream, she told herself. Again and again. But it could easily have happened. Even her nightgown felt hot, as if she'd stood too close to the fire.

She went to the living room, back to the blue armchair. The gigantic dogs upstairs were chasing each other through the night, toenails scraping overhead. She opened her phone. Instantly, an ad came on. A gorgeous woman was getting her wrinkles removed with sound waves. "My husband says I look ten years younger," she said. "Now he acts ten years younger, too!" She winked at Clara.

Another video followed immediately, and another, and another. Spray-on jeans— "Never again fight with that zipper!" House-in-a-Can inflatable furniture, so you never had to worry about friends and loved ones showing up without warning. Fingernail pens you attached to your nails—"Right at your fingertips, or should we say *write* at your fingertips." *Write* was spelled out in loopy cursive. Puffed Lips. Knives that never needed sharpening or your money back. An aid for insomnia—well, that was appropriate. "It works on the principle of opposites," explained a bright-eyed woman who looked well rested. "You trick your brain into thinking you want to stay up, and then you fall asleep! You trick your brain," she kept saying.

Clara knew something about the principle of opposites. What appeared to be an ordinary fifteen-year-old girl could really be someone who was all beaten up and scarred and old, old.

Then an ad came on that she'd never seen before. She tapped her phone to watch the whole thing. It was long. Pale light filled the sky.

PART 3

You Are Here

CHAPTER 21

Rose walked up steps steep as a ladder. The hall smelled of paint though the walls were dirty and peeling. It was Sunday, October 28, late afternoon. She'd gone to brunch and been to the zoo with Cooper, and now she was at Forget-Me-Not, with questions she didn't even know how to ask.

At the top of the stairs was a woman in a neon-green blouse and sharply creased black pants. She had long, rippling gray hair and eyes that matched her blouse, startlingly green.

"I don't know you," Rose said as she climbed. "But your voice . . ."

The lady sighed yet again. "Yes, the voice. That's what people remember, in the cases when they do remember. Or so I'm told."

Rose reached the lady and stood opposite her. Rose was quite a bit taller.

"You're disoriented. That's to be expected too, I suppose.

Well, now that you're here, you . . . might as well come on in."
Though this sounded like it was the last thing she wanted Rose
to do.

Rose followed her through a narrow hall with a wooden
bench. An enormous spider plant hung from a hook in the
ceiling over the bench; if you were sitting there, it would be
practically on top of you. The lady led Rose into an exact cube
of a room and closed the door behind them. More spider plants
were hanging from ceiling hooks. They looked like little alien
invaders, just waiting for you to turn your back so they could
land and finally take over. The smell of paint was everywhere,
but these walls were peeling, too. An overhead light cast a dim
yellow glow, but a tall standing lamp was turned off. The plain
black letters on the window, Forget-Me-Not, were now backward, and curtains at either side billowed even though the
windows were shut tight.

Somehow it seemed important to know more about this
room. Rose pointed to the curtains. "Why are they blowing?"

"The radiator. This is a premillennial building with steam
heating."

"Where's that paint smell coming from?"

"Upstairs. They're converting office space into a dance
studio."

Of course, Rose thought, *there are other businesses in the building.*
But there was something so isolated about this place, like it was
the only business on the planet.

"It's dark," Rose said. "Can I turn on the lamp?"

"Please, don't touch anything! Especially that lamp."

It was like being a kid again on the first day of school, doing everything wrong. There was a gray chair that looked hard, but as soon as Rose sat down, she felt like it could swallow her whole. "This chair," she said, not sure what else to say about it.

"Elephant foam. Our company had it developed specially for our offices. Once you sit, it remembers your body and adjusts to suit your movements. It can handle thousands of customers, or passengers, as the company likes to call them, and it memorizes each one—elephants never forget, of course." She paused. "That's right, you didn't find that so funny last week, either."

"Last week?"

The lady sat in a swivel chair at a glass desk empty except for a wraparound screen and a nameplate that, oddly, was facing her. "Your mother came with you last time. I'm surprised she sent you alone today."

"She doesn't know where I am."

"Isn't she aware of your situation?"

"What situation?"

"That you're here now, of course. That you remembered."

Rose felt like they were going in circles. "Did something happen to me in this room?"

"Let's take a step back." The lady swiveled. "Have you had a blow to the head?"

"No."

"Are you sure? Don't answer too quickly."

Rose hesitated. "No," she said again.

"How about an allergic reaction?"

Rose didn't have allergies, but she gave that question a good, long pause. "No."

"A sudden shock?" No. "Did you jump into a pool of icy water?" No. "Were you given anesthesia?" No. "Even some Novocaine at the dentist's can trigger it."

Rose said she hadn't gone to the dentist, or done anything out of the ordinary.

The lady stopped swiveling. "Strange—it's almost always caused by something external. You must've done it yourself, then. That shows an extraordinary amount of resistance." She frowned at Rose, as if unconvinced that Rose had this in her.

"What have I done?" Rose asked.

"Breakthrough, it's called."

"Breakthrough," Rose repeated. "Isn't that something good?"

"Not in this instance."

Rose pointed out the window. "I had to come here. I was having brunch. I looked up. I'd found a receipt. Of course, that was before." She knew she wasn't explaining it very well.

"But you rang the bell. You could've walked away. I suggested you do just that."

Rose felt herself sink deeper into the chair. It immediately contorted to fit her in a sort of overfamiliar, off-putting way.

"We have many, many satisfied customers who don't even know they're satisfied customers," the lady said. "Don't believe everything you hear about the lawsuits. There are a few unsatisfied people, yes, but well over ninety-five percent of our clients never experience breakthrough or other sort of complication. Even when the proof is right in front of their eyes—looking up and seeing our sign, or finding a receipt, as you say—they'll still deny having it done. Even when they've spent weeks thinking about it, they'll simply assume they've changed their minds. These people aren't lying or crazy. They're just proving it works."

"*What* works?"

The lady widened those startlingly green eyes. "Memory Enhancement. What else are we talking about?"

CHAPTER 22

"Memory Enhancement." Rose just sat there. "Cooper—my friend—knew it. He was right. You . . . you tampered with my memories."

"It's a bit more complicated, Rose. . . . Okay, where do I begin?" The lady paused, as if Rose could help her out, give her a hint. Swiveling in her chair, she glanced at her watch. "Have you got your phone with you? No? Use mine. You need to call your mother so we can get this all straightened out."

"She's my stepmother."

"Yes, of course; she told me your history. Evelyn referred to you as her daughter, just so you know. And you two do look alike—the blue eyes."

The lady's ID pic on her phone showed a yellow parakeet on her shoulder. Rose fastened onto this. "Very cute bird," she said brightly. "At the animal hospital where I work, they don't take parakeets. No exotics. Where do you go when she's sick?"

"It's a *he*. I have a vet who makes home visits, and—" She swiveled some more. "You weren't so chatty last week."

Why am I even talking about birds? Rose wondered. The chair seemed to clamp itself down on her as if she might try to escape. She tapped in Evelyn's number.

"Hello?" Evelyn said tentatively.

"It's me—Rose," she said, in case Evelyn got confused by the unfamiliar ID pic.

"Where are you? Are you okay?" Evelyn's voice shook. "You said you were going out for brunch and coming straight home. Hours went by. You didn't have your phone. I was worried sick. Where are you?"

"I'm at Forget-Me-Not."

There was a pause on the other end. "Oh. So this is Dr. Star's phone? Is she with you?"

Rose looked at the lady. "Are you Dr. Star?"

The lady turned the nameplate around. It said DR. ☆.

"Yes," Rose said into the phone.

"Stay right there. I'm on my way." Evelyn hung up.

"She's on her way, Dr. Star," Rose said.

Dr. Star started swiveling again. "You might as well know, it's not my real name—everyone who works at Forget-Me-Not is Dr. Star. We're affiliated with the practice at the mall in Spruce Hills, called Memory Lane. Everyone there is Dr. Star, too."

"Isn't that kinda awkward? Everyone who comes here meets Dr. Star, so if they tell someone about it later—"

"But that's the point. People don't remember coming

here—at least they're not supposed to." She gave Rose a wary glance. "And nobody else knows about what's happened, either, not husbands or wives or children or friends or coworkers. It was different with your stepmother—she had to know because by law you're a child."

"So you met her. . . ."

"Last Saturday."

"While I was at the zoo," Rose said with some force. "I mean, the Bronx Global Conservation Center."

Dr. Star was shaking her head. "We should wait for your stepmother, but . . . Rose, you were right here with me. Evelyn was in the hall, reading a book. You said your dad had taken you to the zoo when you were a child, so a visit to the zoo was, shall we say, arranged. We're very thorough; we give plenty of visual and auditory cues, animal images and videos, and the brain fills in all the rest—the smell of the animals, maybe the silky feel of alpaca hair at the petting zoo, or the taste of an ice-cream sandwich."

"There was no weather."

"It was a cool fall day with late-afternoon sun. That should've registered."

"The zoo was all wrong today."

"Oh, you actually went to the zoo? That's not good." She *tsk*ed.

"I don't understand." Rose felt dizzy. The chair tightened its grip even more. "What memories were erased? And why would my stepmother force me to do this? I'm happy, finally happy, bursting with happiness."

"Rose—"

"She's always dragging me to doctors and therapists and treatments. They don't work. They're not for me. This couldn't have been my idea."

Dr. Star considered her for a moment. "Well, it was and it wasn't."

The intercom buzzed.

"Goodness, Rose, you only called her five minutes ago! What did she do, fly here?" Dr. Star got up to answer the buzzer, leaving the door wide open behind her.

"I'm here for my daughter," Evelyn said over the intercom, breathlessly.

CHAPTER 23

Rose got up, took a couple of steps, and caught a glimpse of Evelyn out in the hall. Evelyn didn't look well. Her skin was splotchy and raw; her hair, unbelievably, unkempt. And she'd forgotten a book.

Rose, with all her compassion, should've hurried to her stepmother and said a few words, but she couldn't move any closer. Evelyn knew about Forget-Me-Not, about the obliteration of memories. How could Evelyn have done this to her, something so sweeping, so invasive, so . . . what was the word her dad had used about Evelyn?

Everlasting.

Dr. Star came back and closed the door, leaving Evelyn in the hall. "Please sit, Rose. We need to sort you out, help you remember everything. Company policy, should someone find his or her way back to the facility."

Rose still stood there. "Can I sit somewhere else?"

"Everyone loves that chair!" Dr. Star said, sitting in her swivel chair and swiveling. "They want to order one and get frustrated when I tell them they'll never remember even sitting in it."

Rose sank into the chair, which molded itself to her body like a marshmallow with muscle.

"First," Dr. Star said, "you need to be reminded . . . that is, you need to be *told* what it is we do and don't do here. ME— that's what we call Memory Enhancement—is not memory alteration, or erasure, or anything like that. All of your memories, every single one of them, have been and always will be yours."

But that didn't make sense. It did nothing to explain why Rose was so overwhelmingly confused. She did her best to listen carefully, follow every word.

"Memory erasure is, frankly, barbaric. The consequences can be disastrous, with devastating side effects that can be worse than the original memories themselves. Remember Hypno-Friends? Don't get me started on that fiasco. The only memory we actually manipulate is the memory of your visit— three hours, give or take, the trivial amount of time you spend here with us. It's crucial that you don't remember going through the ME procedure. This is because your conscious mind simply wouldn't accept the fact that we can accomplish in hours what usually requires months, if not years, of psychological treatment. No matter the problem, it can be solved as easily as popping a balloon. We can't have you recalling that, can we?

But, once again, all your memories are right where they should be, perfectly preserved. Aside from your memory of last Saturday, that is." She turned her computer screen to face Rose and clicked it on. "Here, this will explain it."

An ad started, in highest res and surround-stereo. It featured a young woman in a red convertible. "I got hit by a car last year and had to get seventeen stitches in my leg," the young woman said cheerfully. "But it was more than a scar. I couldn't drive. I couldn't even cross the street. I just stayed inside my house, a prisoner of fear. Until I went for Memory Enhancement!"

We erase only the pain, flashed across the bottom of the screen. *You'll still be you, with your memories intact . . . a happier you.*

"All it took was one session to give me a whole new outlook. Memory Enhancement doesn't erase or alter the memory of the accident. Imagine the complications! What about my family, my friends, everyone who had seen me in the hospital and in rehab? No, I remember the accident perfectly—Memory Enhancement simply dissociates the emotions I have from the memory itself, and replaces them with serenity and understanding. My new attitude? Accidents happen! No biggie! Of course, I don't remember getting my memory enhanced. I thought I'd spent the day at the gym. Just look at me now," she said, turning the corner, hair streaming in the wind. "Accidents happen!" she called out again with a big smile. "No biggie!"

There were words on a crawl below the woman as she spoke: *Actress portrayal. Based on composite events. Results may vary.*

She had seen this ad before. She'd woken from a nightmare,

gone to the living room, sat in the blue chair, opened her phone, and watched videos for the rest of that night, until it got light outside.

But she hadn't been Rose, then.

"Did I do this?" she said quietly, almost to herself.

"No," answered Dr. Star. "You, Rose, did not."

"So, I mean . . ." God, she was really starting to freak out here. Panic filled her throat, and waves of sadness washed over her, and there was anger, too, coursing through her veins. These feelings so clearly didn't belong to Rose—they had to be connected to something she couldn't remember, despite Dr. Star's insistence. "I had something erased. I must have. Something's missing. Something with . . . my dad?"

"Rose, I promise you. Your father is still there."

She thought about Evelyn in the hall, beneath a low-hanging spider plant. "This had to be my stepmother's idea—so she could take something away from me. It's the only explanation."

"Actually, Rose, your stepmother was concerned and asked me, privately, about side effects and risks. There are none that are statistically significant, as I told her. I don't know how much it helped. She gave her permission, but it was difficult for her—I could see that."

"No, that can't be right." Rose wrapped her arms around herself.

Dr. Star called up another video. "We require proof of consent, in case we need to demonstrate the procedure was done voluntarily."

The video played.

And Rose saw a crystal clear image on the screen, a girl in a flannel shirt and denim overalls; she had limp brown hair with bangs so long you couldn't see her eyes. But you could hear her voice clearly. "I fully understand what's going to happen to me," she said. "I just want to say that I want Memory Enhancement. I want it more than anything. I want it with every cell in my body."

"Do you see now?" Dr. Star said.

I didn't do this, Rose thought, reeling as she recalled what she had known all along. *Clara did.*

Yes. Clara had wanted this, unquestioningly. She'd shaken Evil Lynn awake at dawn, told her to call the nearest Memory Enhancement clinic. A recording said they opened at nine. She'd sat and waited. Evil Lynn had never heard of Memory Enhancement and talked to her, greatly troubled after an hour of researching it online. There were some problems, Evil Lynn had said; it was too new and untested; it was something to think about for a few days and not leap into. But she'd said *Please*, over and over, and when Evil Lynn then said yes, she said *Thank you*. Finally, the office opened. What luck—she could go that afternoon; they'd had a cancellation. Why would anyone cancel anything so miraculous? Don't plan to do anything afterward, she was told—you'll just sleep and sleep. Evil Lynn tried to get her to eat breakfast. She wasn't a bit hungry. Evil Lynn asked if she wanted to sleep a few hours. She couldn't lie still. She carefully went over the route there on her phone, again and again, memorizing the names of streets, even visualizing all the turns. On the walk over, she didn't have to refer to the phone once; she could've made the trip in her sleep. Evil Lynn kept asking if she was absolutely sure about this.

Yes, Clara was absolutely sure. Because the woman in the red convertible had actually done it.

She had changed places with herself.

CHAPTER 24

"You were given a shot of Alitrol," Dr. Star said.

"Yes, on my jaw." She pointed to the spot. "It's been hurting all week."

"Unrelated. The needle we use is tiny and doesn't even leave a mark."

"Maybe you hit a nerve."

Dr. Star tightened her lips.

Had Rose just hit a nerve here, too? "If I was a frog, that spot would be my tympanum."

Dr. Star shrugged at that and turned her screen back to face her. "Last week, the special light we use plus the Alitrol put you into a state we call IT—Irresistible Trance."

"A trance," Rose said. Clara's life in the glass coffin had been a kind of trance. Had she traded in that trance for a new one?

"It is most certainly not a parlor trick. Just like the woman in the ad said, Memory Enhancement is a proven technology that works with a person's own memories and realigns the emotions attached to those memories. That's all." Dr. Star peered at her computer. "I've never dealt with a case like this before, though it's part of the training, of course. Here we are, breakthrough, blue light . . ." She took a few moments to read, and then she gestured toward the tall standing lamp. "We use the red light during ME, which gives the room a lovely glow."

"Red light—I see it when I wake up."

"That has been reported in extremely rare cases, as well. Harmless and temporary," she added with emphasis. "Now, the blue light; that's what we need to use in case of breakthrough." She got up, fiddled with the lamp. "Wait, I have to change the setting—it's stuck. My first time doing this— There!" She clicked it on.

Rose had to adjust to the light, the color of the ocean when a storm approaches. At first she thought maybe she was seeing things behind her eyelids, but she was blinking, which meant her eyes must be open. She felt she was half awake, half asleep, and half something else . . . but that was too many halves. . . . Would she be waking up to blue light from now on?

"Does the light affect you, too?" she asked.

"I wear special contacts," Dr. Star replied.

"So your eyes aren't really green?"

"They are not." Dr. Star sounded a little disappointed. "Now, I'll walk you through it. You will remember things as I tell them to you. We began by talking about memory, which we hold sacred here at Forget-Me-Not; we honor and cherish it. Without memory, one philosopher said, we'd be no better than a looking glass, constantly receiving images and reflecting them back, never the better or worse for it."

"You mean mirror."

"It was a quote, Rose; no one says 'looking glass' anymore. Memory molds our personalities, shapes our possibilities, lends depth to our consciousness, depth like the buried cities near Mount Vesuvius, one on top of the other, the present cities on top of increasingly long-ago ruins of cities."

"I tried talking to Mr. Slocum about Mount Vesuvius. He didn't want to hear it."

Dr. Star ignored this and adjusted the lamp.

The blue light seemed to intensify, as if the ocean was darkening, or maybe her eyes were playing tricks on her.

Dr. Star's teeth looked like smooth glowing stones. "When a person suffers a terrible experience, the memory is seared into the brain. From an evolutionary standpoint, this is beneficial. Next time there's a challenge to be faced, she'll remember what happened, remain alert, and handle things better. But in some cases the memory is as fresh as the trauma itself and doesn't diminish over time. It's like a dog that keeps bringing the pain back to you, wagging its tail. The young woman in the car? She put it all behind her. Accidents happen! In your case— your father died seven years ago, and you weren't, shall we say, moving on?" Dr. Star smiled briefly; was that kindness shining through? "Here is the beauty, the art of Memory Enhancement. While the red light is on and Alitrol is in your system, we come

up with new perspectives, new feelings to attach to your memories, to your sense of yourself. Think of it as a salad bar. You
pick and choose. A slice of cucumber, a tomato wedge, a radish
flower."

Yes. Clara had wanted so much. She was starving.

"Best to narrow it down, I told you. You can't take everything; your plate would be overfull and you would never finish.
We chose happiness, of course. Every day was like a gift you
didn't need to unwrap. If sadness reared its ugly head, I told you
there's no sadness, no need for it; if anger flared up, it could be
banished like a bad king, never to return. You said you had no
friends, that you had one long ago but she was lost to you now. I
said that once you became happy, bursting with happiness, you
would find yourself with lots of friends, the old one and many
new ones, and do all kinds of fun things together, and have a
boyfriend, too, why not? Most of all, you wanted to live your
life fully, not sit at the bus stop and miss the bus or some such
thing. I told you that you were at the center of your life, not the
edge. Oh, and you had to love animals."

"Because the girl in the jean jacket had a dog. She'd put a
sweater on the dog."

Dr. Star shook her head. "You kept saying, 'Make me like
her'—even though she was a stranger."

But to Clara the girl in the jean jacket wasn't a stranger. Clara
knew her through and through, inside and out.

"I asked you to come up with a new name or nickname for
yourself; that often helps the enhanced person seal the deal.

You latched onto Rose immediately. 'My name is Rose,' you said. 'I am Rose Hartel.'"

Of course she was Rose. On the back of the jean jacket, for all the world to see, there was an embroidered rose, lovingly sewn by the girl's mother.

"Then you took a virtual visit to the zoo. It was Rose who saw the animals; Rose had a perfectly wonderful time. You were so eager to have people call you by your new name. I specifically told your stepmother it would help things along if she called you Rose. I wonder if she decided not to—?"

"She called me Rose."

Dr. Star snapped off the blue light.

"You were happy, Rose, weren't you?"

"I still am," she said, in her despair.

CHAPTER 25

"Dr. Star," she said, "you have to fix this."

"Mm?"

"I can't—I don't know—"

"Rose. Take a deep breath."

She did, but it felt like no air entered her lungs. "So what happens now? Do we just reverse the procedure?" *I'll simply go back into the glass coffin,* she thought.

"There's no reversing it. I am sorry."

She thought she hadn't heard Dr. Star correctly. "You're sorry . . . about what?"

"Reversal isn't possible, Rose. It's not as though we removed pieces of you like books out of a library, and we can just put them back on the shelves. We fundamentally altered your physiological responses to your memories."

No reversal . . . fundamentally altered . . . What had been done to her? What was she going to do with the feelings Rose wasn't even supposed to have, now or ever again? "Dr. Star . . . what's me and what's ME?"

"I don't follow—"

"Okay. . . . Okay. We can't reverse it." She breathed more giant gulps of air, as Dr. Star had instructed her to do. Why wasn't the air getting to where it was supposed to go? "Just do it again," she said finally. "Put on the red light—let's pick new things from the salad bar. . . ."

"Rose, it's not so simple."

"You have to!" she cried out. And then, more softly: "Please, I need the red light." Oh God. The blue light had turned her into a crazy person. A couple of years ago, walking on Belle Heights Drive, a woman heading toward her was yelling non-stop, cursing up a storm. But when she passed Clara, she looked right at her and said sweetly, "Have a nice day, darlin'."

"There is an option available, upon request." Dr. Star was scrutinizing something on her computer.

"What is it? What?"

"A refresher. It's not a 'fix,' but it might help. We can reinforce the idea that you never had Memory Enhancement."

"Yes. Good."

"You'll remember that you tried it once but it didn't take. It'll become a casual anecdote of your past. You'll tell people you went for Memory Enhancement but it didn't work—because of your exceptional strength."

"Sure, okay, fine." *Get on with it,* she thought. It was too much for her, what she was feeling on one side, and who she was supposed to be on the other. *Rose.*

"We won't use the zoo this time, and we'll put a special emphasis on the weather, maybe double your dose of Alitrol—"

"Triple it." She leaned back into the elephant foam. "I'm ready."

Dr. Star frowned. "We have to wait at least seventy-two hours."

She felt the color drain from her face. "No! It has to be now!" She tried to lower her voice. "Is it the money? I have a job, I'll pay, even if it takes a really long time."

"It's not that, Rose. Refreshers are actually free if breakthrough occurs within two weeks. Listen to me carefully. You know how when you get a perma-braid, you can't do anything to your hair for several days?"

"This has nothing to do with my hair." She put some hair behind one ear but not the other.

"Just an example," Dr. Star said. "After a perma-braid, your hair needs to rest. You've just been under the blue light. Your brain needs to rest."

"It's rested."

"I don't make the rules, Rose."

"Okay"—she counted on her fingers—"that's Wednesday. I'll stay here until then."

"Excuse me?"

"The chair won't mind." She patted the arms.

"Rose, we have other clients."

"I'll wait in the other room. I won't be in the way."

"You can't just *live* here, Rose. Besides, I said at least seventy-two hours, which means, more precisely, Thursday. Which isn't available," she said quickly. "We're booked solid. The earliest we have is Saturday, two p.m."

"A week—a whole week?"

"More like six days. And today is nearly over, isn't it?"

No, today wasn't nearly over—there was the whole evening to get through, and the night, the long night. "Wait, I have an idea. What about Memory Lane in Spruce Hills? Maybe they can see me Thursday."

Dr. Star took a deep breath. "There have been some . . . issues at Memory Lane. It's closed. Temporarily. Saturday, two p.m. is the earliest. It might not be me that day but a different Dr. Star. Do you still want the appointment?"

"Totally."

"Well, I just thought, because you and I have gotten to know each other, you might want to wait for my availability."

God, no! she almost shouted, but—did Dr. Star sound a little hurt? Someone who was kind and had a big heart might think so. "I'd prefer you, but it would be really, really hard to wait longer. Is that okay?"

"I understand perfectly." Dr. Star looked satisfied. She got up, opened the door, and gestured for Evelyn to come inside.

Evelyn reached out for her, but she stepped back.

"Oh, she'll settle down!" Dr. Star said. "The blue light—it can be like taking an ocean voyage. A bit of seasickness might set in."

Seasick? More like thrown overboard and drowning. But—there was a life raft to cling to. It had letters on the side: *Saturday two p.m.* She just had to hold on until then.

Dr. Star and Evelyn spoke for a few minutes about the return visit. "No charge," Dr. Star said, but Evelyn did not look pleased about coming back for the refresher. "We'll need you to bring her in and take her home."

"Of course," Evelyn said, "if that's what you really want, Rose. Or is it Clara?"

"Best if you continue to go by Rose." Dr. Star turned to her. "Clara belongs to the past. But you, Rose—you have a future."

CHAPTER 26

Outside, the girl—which was how she couldn't help thinking of herself—felt even more unsteady. Who was she now, no-longer-Clara, not-yet-Rose? She was too full of blanks, like an unsolved crossword puzzle. The biggest blank of all—

Her name. She didn't even know how many letters it was supposed to have.

It didn't help that the sidewalk had the most enormous, treacherous-looking cracks, like something left by an earth-quake—how could Rose not have noticed them? If the girl wasn't careful, she could come crashing down.

Evelyn kept pace with her, even when the girl walked slower or sped up.

She's practically breathing down my neck.

"You must be hungry," Evelyn said.

True, the girl had to eat. This was something that needed to be done between now and Saturday, two p.m. Rose would want something new and exciting, something to make her taste buds dance. Clara, on the other hand, would've been fine with stale bread.

"How does pasta primavera sound?" Evelyn put a hand on the girl's shoulder, trying to get her to stop. The girl kept going. "Listen, I just want to say, if you'd like to talk about it—"

"I'll eat in my room, if it's all the same to you," the girl said evenly.

Evelyn said, "I understand."

She wasn't asking for *understanding*, especially not from Evelyn.

At home she went straight to her room and grabbed the bald elephant. She looked at it carefully, trying to imagine her mother doing the same thing. But she couldn't. Her dad used to read to her in this room. She rummaged around inside herself, wanting to feel what Clara had felt, and not felt, all that time in the glass coffin, after suddenly losing her dad, and not having Kim, either, and living with Evil Lynn all those years. She had Clara's memories, of course, but because of the Memory Enhancement, so much of Clara was gone forever. The girl felt a pang for this previous self she would never really know—a pang Rose hadn't felt, it occurred to her. Well, maybe Rose hadn't gotten around to it yet.

But Rose reached out to people who seemed alone. Shouldn't the girl somehow try to feel closer to Clara, a lost soul if ever there was one?

That, as Rose would say, was as worthy a project as any.

In the meantime, she picked up her phone. An ad came on for antiaging skin care. Poor Clara, there wasn't an antiaging ingredient in the world strong enough to penetrate her inner self. The girl swiped the ad away and tapped the calculator. It was seven p.m., so there were five hours until midnight, then five twenty-four-hour days until midnight Friday, and add twelve to get to noon on Saturday, plus two more final hours until two p.m. Total: 139 hours. Then of course each hour had sixty minutes, so there were 8,340 minutes, or 500,400 seconds before the red light would get turned on. She kept recalculating and watching the numbers, emerging and disappearing, in a cold, detached sequence.

The girl ate two full plates of pasta at the desk in her room. She slept through the night—with the light on.

Monday morning the girl woke to the *hoo-hoo*-ing of birds on Mrs. Moore's windowsill. They sounded genuinely heartbroken. Memory Enhancement for birds—it was something Dr. Lola could start offering. The tagline was obvious—birds *hoo-hoo*-ing before and *ha-ha*-ing after.

Then she realized—the red light was gone. No blue light, either.

The girl had to get ready for school.

In the shower, which soap to use? Clara would've chosen the unscented soap; Rose had used Evelyn's. Or should there be a third bar of soap? This was ridiculous, facing paralysis over soap. She closed her eyes and reached for a bar—which turned out to be Evelyn's. Fine. The same thing with clothes—just grab a few things without looking and put them on. She ended up in blue pants and an old sweatshirt. She didn't wear lipstick. She tucked some hair behind one ear and not the other.

At school, the halls felt small and stuffed with jostling, bellowing kids. One of them was talking about how Dylan Beck got in trouble last year on Halloween—"showing up in his underwear as the Invisible Man who didn't know he wasn't invisible." But she noticed a girl with the most gorgeous purple hair. She couldn't help stopping her, putting a hand on her arm, and saying, "Your hair is fantastic—it's like the scent of lavender got captured in a hair color." Oh God, should she have said that? But the purple-haired girl looked thrilled, which gave the girl a thrill, too.

Outside homeroom, Selena rushed up to her. "So this Saturday I booked you a DJ! Isn't that great?"

"Huh?"

"Don't you remember? You promised. At brunch." Selena jabbed an elbow into her ribs.

The girl saw that Selena had deep frown lines between her eyebrows. Rose had thought Selena was always cheerful and smiling. "This Saturday?"

Selena narrowed her eyes. "What's wrong with this Saturday?"

The girl remembered how much Rose had needed to sleep last weekend, all the rest of Saturday and until two o'clock Sunday. With the extra Alitrol she might sleep clear through to Monday. "How about the weekend after? I'll be ready by then."

"I'm gonna pretend I didn't hear that. This party is *on*." She turned around and said over her shoulder, "Here's your chance to actually get with Nick again. Don't blow it like last time!"

In the cafeteria, the girl picked up a sesame-seed bagel, oatmeal-raisin cookies in a pack, and pineapple juice sticks.

At the scanner, Cooper had a little glint in his eyes—beautiful eyes, brown with flecks of green. But that unibrow—ugh. "Hey, how you doing? Want to talk later, about what happened at Forget-Me-Not?"

She shook her head. "Nothing happened, as it turned out."

"Your memory—?"

"Wasn't tampered with." Wait, Dr. Star had told her what her new cover story would be. "I mean, I tried Memory Enhancement, but it didn't work. So that's the end of that." She put her money on the counter.

"Are you sure? It really seemed like something happened—"

"I'm totally fine. I don't have any more pain in my jaw, either." She'd forgotten all about that, until now. "Turns out I got a shot there. Maybe it went too deep."

"Ouch." He made a face. "Hey, we got lucky. This Sunday, *Ball of Fire* is coming to You Must Remember This."

For a second she forgot that *Ball of Fire* was a screwball comedy; it sounded like a plummeting meteor. "Sunday . . . I can't, I can't."

He looked really disappointed. "It's only playing that one day."

"I have to sleep—I don't know for how long."

"Really? Can't think of a better excuse?"

"I'm handling it the best I can," she said, "under the circumstances."

"What circumstances?"

"Here." She shoved the money toward him.

"Jeez, Louise, are we having our first fight?"

It sounded exactly like something her dad would've said. "It's not Louise. It was never Louise."

"I'm kidding. I'm just kidding." The glint in his eyes grew dimmer.

The girl sat by herself at her old corner table with its view of a brick wall, which darkened within minutes, soaked by a sudden driving rain. The air in the cafeteria changed, too, and got heavy and damp with a smell of leaves and dust. Rain spattered the window. Nobody looked up, but didn't they understand that something outside had seeped into the inside? She took out her phone, bypassing the ID pic, and went straight to the calculator. It was Monday, noon, so there were now five full twenty-four-hour days until Saturday noon, plus two more hours.

"Good for you—you're not out with Thing One and Thing Two," the girl heard over her shoulder, and looked up to see Kim in a football referee shirt. Kim pulled up a chair, opened the girl's pack of cookies, and helped herself to one. "I ate already but I'm still hungry." She snapped off a piece of a juice stick and popped it into her mouth. She peered over at the girl's phone. "New puzzle?"

"I'm counting down," she said, too quickly.

"To what?"

The girl hesitated. Kim was her friend, her old friend, her new friend, the friend who'd put makeup on her, and why, exactly, had Clara agreed to do that? It had led only to trouble. "Nothing."

"Counting down to nothing? You realize you're not making sense."

"I just have to get through the next few days. Okay? Why is everybody on me about it?"

"Rose, you could tell me, you know. When we were kids, we called each other cross-my-heart friends."

The girl took a breath. Kim wasn't making this easy. "Just . . . give me until next week. We'll do a puzzle. We'll have lots of fun."

"Next week?" Kim sounded hurt. "You don't want to hang out in the meantime?"

"Please. It's better that way."

Kim had taken another cookie out of the pack, but she put it back.

CHAPTER 27

In bio lab the girl saw Nick Winter, diagonally in front of her, two tables over. Clara had barely noticed him; Rose had thought he was the most gorgeous thing ever. Now she gave him a steady, intense look that he must've felt, because he turned to glance at her. His expression was a complete blank.

He didn't remember anything at all, she realized—dancing with her, kissing her. Did he even remember the party, or much about his life? If you had no memory, you couldn't get it enhanced; there'd be nothing to work on. He was still really good-looking, though, even without a memory.

During class Mr. Slocum announced, "Miss Hartel, please report to Ms. Pratt."

What was that all about? She hadn't done anything.

"You'd better not be in trouble," Selena whispered fiercely. "Your mother might punish you and cancel the party. I've already invited everybody."

When the girl got to Ms. Pratt's office, the door was open. Ms. Pratt, in a beige pantsuit and with her hair in a bun on top of her head, was facing the other way.

"I don't understand," the girl said.

Ms. Pratt turned around. She held a baby in her arms. "My wife had to drop him off, and I remembered you wanted to see him."

Out of nowhere, another impossible decision. She wanted to hold him; she wanted to get away as fast as she could.

"Want a better look?"

"I can see him from here."

"Come on! Do I need to pull you along?" Ms. Pratt laughed as the girl took a few steps forward. "Now, put your hand under his head and hold his body with your other arm. Good!"

The baby was much heavier than he looked. He had a lot of eyelashes that were thick and distinct; she could see each separate one. He smelled soft and powdery. He was like a warm bundle of possibility.

"Ethan likes you," Ms. Pratt said.

"Babies like everybody."

"You'd be surprised. Whenever he sees my mother, he bursts into tears. But then, so do I." She laughed again. "He's so relaxed with you. No fear at all."

The girl kept hold of Ethan, sure that he would sense the turmoil within and burst into tears, too. But he just gazed at her with big brown eyes.

* * *

The girl had to go back to bio lab and pick up her stuff. There was Mr. Slocum at his computer. Something stirred in her, quick as lightning, an all-over kind of ache. She wasn't sure what it was. If she was doing a crossword puzzle, lots of long words might fit. Isolation. Alienation. Loneliness.

This was what Clara had felt and not felt.

She was about to leave when she heard herself say, "Excuse me."

Mr. Slocum looked up.

She could feel the seconds tick away—which was good, because each moment gone brought Saturday, two p.m., closer. But you simply did not waste Mr. Slocum's time, even so. "Last week, I asked you a bunch of questions. You said I was full of myself. Wow, you have no idea. But it went wrong that time. There was no weather, I saw a red light, though that's gone and I hope for good, too. So I owe you an apology. For prying into, you know, your life."

Outside, trees rustled in a strong breeze. Mr. Slocum gave her a curt nod. "Something went wrong?"

"I had Memory Enhancement." Oh, she could kick herself! No one was supposed to know.

"Memory Enhancement—should I have heard of that? Is that one of those newfangled memory replacement things?"

"No, it's not a replacement, but—well, there was this girl in a jean jacket. She wanted to be just like her."

"She?"

"What I wanted, I mean. Not sure I completely understand

it. I should understand it, shouldn't I? Maybe if I saw that girl in the jean jacket again—" Actually, she realized, this could help her connect to Clara, close up some of that distance between them. "I've taken up way too much of your time, Mr. Slocum."

"It's fine, Miss Hartel. I would tell you if you were bothering me. You said something about not understanding?"

"Thanks so much, Mr. Slocum. Bye." She rushed out the door.

The girl sat on a backless bench at the Q22/24 bus stop, opposite a Food-A-Rama, and unlike everyone else purposely faced the sidewalk, not the street, where the buses, sooner or later, would appear. But she had a great view of the people walking by. She scanned the midafternoon crowds for a girl in a jean jacket with a rose embroidered on the back.

Though with this chill in the air, she might be wearing a heavier coat, or already have on a Halloween costume, on her way to a party. Maybe her dog was home. It was simpler just to look for someone with very dark hair, chin-length, with one side tucked behind one ear. Then she could go up to her and say, "Can I talk to you?" Even if the dark-haired girl were in a hurry, she'd stop awhile, because that was the kind of person she was. The girl would ask the things Clara had wanted to know: "Please, tell me about your family, your friends, your day-to-day life."

And, "What's your name?"

The sky turned deep violet-blue with glowing silver clouds.

The girl breathed in cold air and saw her breath come out in sharp puffs. Nobody spoke to her except for a lady who told her to turn around, dear, because the bus had just arrived. "That's okay," the girl said. "I'll wait for the next one." She put in her earbuds and listened to "Changes." By the time she decided to head for home, she was 116 hours away from Saturday, two p.m. She hadn't seen the dark-haired girl yet, but she would come back tomorrow, and the day after, if she had to, and the day after that.

CHAPTER 28

"Miss Hartel, see me after class," Mr. Slocum said on Tuesday.

This made no sense. What had she done this time? Besides, she had to go back to the bus stop right away. She'd kept close vigil all through lunch; she still hadn't seen the girl in the jean jacket.

When bio class ended, she swallowed hard and went to Mr. Slocum's desk.

"Miss Hartel, you owe me some time for school service."

What was he talking about? At least, she noticed, his head wasn't turning purple, the way it usually did when he was angry. "I did the six hours," she said quietly.

"How about all that time you talked my ear off? I deducted it." He got up and dragged over one of the student chairs. "Have a seat."

She placed herself on the edge of the chair.

"You asked me about myself." Mr. Slocum went back to his desk, sat, and opened a drawer. "I brought a photo album." It was an old-fashioned leather loose-leaf binder, just color pictures in clear plastic sleeves. He pointed to a brownstone. "This is where I was born, in Red Hook, Brooklyn. That tall boy next to me is my brother, Eugene. He teaches chemistry." There was Mr. Slocum in high school, a basketball player with long straight hair down to his shoulders, and in college, and getting married. He was widowed now. He was displaying his life for her, only the broadest strokes, of course, but he must know she could tell everybody about this and get a good laugh.

When he was finished, he drew himself up. "You have now fulfilled your school service, Clara."

Not Miss Hartel. Clara.

"I did a little reading on Memory Enhancement. You don't lose your memories, but you feel altogether differently about them, have I got that right?"

She nodded, impressed. He understood ME very well.

"Sometimes people change their name, I hear. It is still Clara, isn't it?"

"Close enough," she said, the simplest answer. Of all the teachers she'd ever had, how come horrible Mr. Slocum had been the only one to notice something off about her? He'd called it la-la land—which was also close enough, since he had no way of knowing about a glass coffin. He'd been a jerk about it, too. Well, until today.

"Really, thank you," she said.

"Don't mention it."

"Oh, I wouldn't! Wait, you mean—okay, right."

She grabbed her things. She'd thought she would rush to the bus stop but found herself walking slowly for no reason she could think of. It was as if she wasn't sure how to get there and didn't want to take a wrong turn and get lost.

Once at the bus stop, she did homework for the rest of the afternoon, looking up every few moments so she wouldn't miss the dark-haired girl, and hearing the sighs of the hydro-buses as they came and went. She wasn't getting much work done because she also kept checking the time—ninety-four hours to go, ninety-three, ninety-two.

At one point her phone buzzed. Cooper had sent her a link, and a message:

Hope to see you, where or when.

She tapped on the link; it was that song "Where or When." She popped in her earbuds. It was beautiful. But she just played it once.

All afternoon she saw only one person she recognized: Ms. Brackman, who had Candy with her. Candy plopped down on the sidewalk not far from the bus stop and for several minutes absolutely would not budge from the spot.

"Don't be like that!" Ms. Brackman said, before opening her handbag and taking out a piece of chicken.

Wednesday lunch and afternoon found her back at the bus stop. It was Halloween, and tons of kids were in costumes:

superheroes, firefighters, Mr. and Ms. Potato Heads. Still, there was no girl in the jean jacket. It was as if the dark-haired girl was deliberately avoiding her.

She was just hauling out some books when her phone buzzed. There was a message from Dr. Lola:

Short-staffed today can u walk Rouge?

This was so inconsiderate—she needed to sit here. Why couldn't Dr. Lola just leave her alone? What was it about having a blissful, carefree childhood that made someone think she could snap her fingers and get what she wanted?

The girl could still hear Dr. Star's flat, generic voice: *There's no anger, it's gone, like a banished king, never to return.*

But the anger, like a lake of lava seething inside her, lingered.

From deep, deep down, this was Clara's anger, erupting.

On my way, she texted back. It occurred to the girl that, after all, Dr. Lola might be doing her a favor. The girl in the jean jacket might be at the dog run.

Gr8!!! Dr. Lola answered. *What's with the ID pic?*

Well, it wasn't something you could explain in a text.

At the animal hospital, Stacey greeted her with a smile. "You're a lifesaver! Dr. Lola's in the back."

The girl walked down the hall and found Dr. Lola cleaning a dog's teeth. Rose had seen this procedure. You had to sedate the dog. The dog lies on its back on a long, shiny table, eyes open but unseeing, here but not here.

Like Clara in the glass coffin. But the psychic had said it to Rose, not Clara, that she was "here but not here." Which had confused Rose and confused the girl now, too.

"Rose, thank you so much!" Dr. Lola said, turning around and taking off her gloves. Rouge ran over to the girl and immediately tucked her chin down and pushed the top of her head into the girl's side.

"Where'd Rouge come from?" she asked.

"She's a rescue," Dr. Lola said. "She wound up in a shelter for abused and abandoned animals."

Poor Rouge. What had she been through? No way to ever know, either; it wasn't as though Rouge could pull a photo album out of a desk drawer.

Out on the sidewalk the girl noticed something Rose hadn't picked up on, that people hurried out of her way now that she had an enormous dog at her side. It made her feel powerful, but also uncomfortable, because people didn't understand. She wanted to say, *Don't be afraid—she's a pussycat!*

The dog run in Belle Heights Park was a dusty oval surrounded by a five-foot-high fence. The benches along the perimeter weren't even half full. A sign on the gate at the entrance said No Dogs Without People; No People Without Dogs. It had the ring of authority. It could be the eleventh commandment.

The girl watched Rouge run around with a couple of dachshunds, a golden retriever, a few poodles, and an Australian cattle dog, a kind of dog she'd first seen at the animal hospital.

Dr. Lola had talked about how these dogs were a fairly new breed, a cross between collies and wild dogs—dingoes.

But there was no small dog in a sweater, no girl in the jean jacket. Every few minutes, Rouge came back to her for a pat on the head. Luckily, the girl had a bottle of water in her backpack. She cupped some water in her hands and let Rouge have a drink.

At one point the Australian cattle dog jumped up on the bench next to her. It was compact and muscular, with a short silvery coat, upright ears, and black patches on its face. It stared right at her with golden eyes. Clara would've been terrified. Rose had loving trust in animals. But the girl felt something else—a kinship with this dog who was still part wild and probably had a lot of conflicting stuff going on. If she were to get a dog, this was the kind of dog she would get.

Somebody threw a Frisbee. The dog leaped off the bench and caught it in midair.

The sky went from bright sunshine to pearly gray-blue to deep blue. Several planes whooshed by, and in the distance she heard fire trucks wailing—how many, three, four? What an amazing thing to do with your life, she thought, rescue people trapped in burning buildings.

"What do you think, Rouge?" she asked as they walked back on curvy streets. "Should I become a firefighter?" Of course that would put her in a uniform, not a costume.

Rouge grew fixated on a squirrel clinging motionless upside down on the trunk of an oak tree. It seemed to be giving Rouge the evil eye, knowing it was safely out of reach.

* * *

"So," Dr. Lola said, when they got back, "see you Saturday?"

"Saturday—I'm sorry, I can't," the girl said. "I have to have a medical procedure."

Dr. Lola took a step closer. "Nothing serious, I hope?"

"Oh, no, totally routine. But I'll make up the time. I'll work both days the weekend after."

"Don't worry; we'll figure something out."

There were sixty-eight hours to go. Or was it sixty-seven? She'd lost count, temporarily.

When she got home, there was a painting about two feet square she'd never seen before, leaning against the wall in the living room. A Post-it said: *Mrs. Moore wanted you to have this. She had it in her closet and doesn't have enough wall space to hang it up.*

The girl knew that wasn't true. She'd been up there; Mrs. Moore had plenty of wall space. If she accepted the painting, she'd have to talk to Mrs. Moore and listen to all her little stories—she had no time for that now. She went upstairs to return the painting, and knocked.

The dogs were there, scuffling and huffing behind the door, but Mrs. Moore wasn't home. The girl couldn't very well leave the painting in the landing or leaning on the front door, so she brought it back downstairs, to her room.

And looked at it.

Rose had found these paintings just a smear of colors. But the girl could see how they made sense. The browns and grays

194

here, the big rectangles and little squares, were so clearly the apartment houses and the five-story building across the way, the view from Clara's childhood, the block as it had been before Belle Heights Tower. It looked as though Mr. Moore had painted it while looking out at the world through a thick pane of glass, as if he'd painted this for her alone.

At her desk, the girl sat at her computer and typed a letter. She didn't even know what she'd written until she read it over:

> *Thank you for the painting. I put it in my room, where I can see it every night last thing and every morning first thing. If you ever want to look at it again, please come downstairs anytime. I'm sorry I never got the chance to meet your husband.*
>
> *Yours truly, your neighbor*

She printed it out, folded it in half, went upstairs, and slid it under Mrs. Moore's door. She heard the dogs again and told them sternly, "Don't rip that up! It's not for you."

That night the moon cast pale-gray light over Belle Heights Tower. The girl was again hunched over her phone, watching ads, as Clara used to do. Liquid Lenses—to replace unwieldy glasses and messy contact lenses. She swiped it away. A mattress with a built-in alarm that gently nudged you awake. Swipe. Movable tattoos. Swipe. Towels that absorbed water and stayed dry to the touch. Swipe. Memory Enhancement . . . there was the woman in the red car, calling herself "a prisoner of fear."

Clara had always felt as though she was the only person in the world watching these things in the middle of the night. But of course Clara wasn't the only one, far from it; there were millions of ads playing around the clock for millions of people—all of whom, like her, had been specifically targeted. What were all these other people like, she wondered now, what were they hoping to find? Maybe they were people who knew life wasn't fair and were trying to change the odds.

No wonder it was such a huge business.

By the time she went to sleep, she realized there were only about sixty hours to go. Saturday, two p.m. was getting much, much closer. So why did it feel like it was moving further away?

CHAPTER 29

Thursday afternoon she sat at the bus stop and imagined the conversation she would have with the girl in the jean jacket. Maybe they'd get along so well they'd want to talk again, about deeper things, hopes and dreams. They'd exchange phone numbers and—

Wait. There was that ID pic on her phone. Something needed to be done about that, right away.

A few minutes later she pressed the buzzer in the lobby of Belle Heights Tower.

"Yeah?" Kim said over the intercom.

"It's me," the girl said.

"It's you, all right. But it's not next week yet."

The girl faced the camera. "This is kinda important. Can I come up?"

Kim buzzed her in. The girl got on the elevator and pressed fourteen. A gray-haired man got on with her, pressed nine, and said pleasantly, "It's cold, it's muggy, it's sunny, it's raining . . . when will the weather make up its mind?"

Small talk. Clara would've kept her head down, bangs over her eyes, silent. Rose would've engaged the man in lively conversation. The girl glanced over at him and said, "It's really weird when there's no weather at all."

He gave her kind of a look before getting out on his floor.

Outside the elevator she was greeted by Kim, her hair unbraided and covering her shoulders like a thick, glossy blanket. The girl had forgotten that Kim had fantastic hair. Everyone thought Astrid had the best hair in the grade, but clearly she didn't.

The girl followed Kim down the hall, through the living room, and past the bathroom with the fuzzy blue toilet-seat cover. This time they went to Kim's room, which was an utter mess. Piles of books and papers and clothes were everywhere, along with scattered notes and slapdash but surprisingly vivid sketches of people with green skin, white cows with large brown spots, and furry gray wolves.

"Great drawings."

"They're possible ideas for *Into the Woods*. I'm having so much fun with it." Kim plopped down on her bed, on top of a mass of T-shirts, and gestured for the girl to sit in the straight-backed wooden chair at her desk, which only had a few sweaters draped over it.

The girl folded the sweaters neatly and put them on top of Kim's dresser. She'd always been good at this. Kim's window looked down on a parking lot. The whoosh of traffic and honk-ing cars on Belle Heights Expressway was actually louder here than in the girl's apartment. "So, why I'm here." The girl sat on the wooden chair. "Can I trust you, Kim, as a cross-my-heart friend?"

"Of course," Kim said, as if it was the most obvious thing in the world.

"I'm going to tell you something, and you have to promise not to tell anybody. People who've done this—no one can ever know about it, not husbands or wives or children or coworkers."

Kim threw a pillow at her. It arced and landed softly on her lap. "I promise not to tell your children."

"*Kim*. It's not funny. There's one person you must especially never, ever tell."

"And who's that?"

The girl threw the pillow directly back with a little force. "Me."

The girl told Kim everything; Kim had never heard of Memory Enhancement.

"Dr. Star said I had extraordinary resistance," the girl said. "My dad thought I was strong willed. My stepmother called it a stubborn streak. A rose by any other name, you know?" She'd had no intention of saying anything to anyone else, either blurt-ing it out like she did with Mr. Slocum, or deliberately, as she was doing now. But she wanted Kim's help. "I have to go back for a refresher, this Saturday at two p.m. Rose mustn't remember my second visit to Forget-Me-Not. So you can't say anything to trigger it. It's my last chance—I don't think they'd let her back another time."

"You're talking about yourself in the third person, you know," Kim said.

"Huh? I'm a *third* person?"

"No, I mean you're using the he/she voice about yourself, Rose."

"Oh." But it stuck in her craw a little, as her dad used to say, this idea of someone else entirely. Wasn't she crowded enough already? "Kim, there's something else I need to ask. Please take my picture again. I know it sounds kinda crazy, but I have to find this girl. She wears a jean jacket with a large embroidered rose on the back. She's got dark hair, chin length, and really red lipstick. Have you seen her around?"

"Well," Kim said, "I see someone who looks a lot like her."

The girl straightened her back. "Anyway. I sit at the bus stop and look around. It's the best place to see lots of people."

"You sit at the bus stop—like the beat-up old woman I created when I put makeup on you?"

"This is completely different. I'm waiting for the girl in the jean jacket, so I can talk to her a little. What if she wants to call me sometime? I can't have that ID pic popping up."

Kim got out her phone. "Sure, I'll take your picture."

The girl beamed before erasing the smile altogether. Kim kept clicking away and then scrolled through what she'd shot. "Don't like that smile *at all* . . . or that one . . . here you look like you're gonna slug someone. . . . Hey, I like this one. Your eyes look sad, though. Take a look."

It was a good picture. The girl wasn't smiling but she wasn't not-smiling, either. Kim was right about the eyes. There was sadness there, deep and raw. In a big box of crayons, the color could be called Sad Blue.

Kim sent the image to the girl's phone, where she slotted it in as her ID pic. As for the old, old woman, she put that in a new file, undeleted.

"I should get back to the bus stop," the girl said.

Kim walked her to the elevator and pressed the down button. "Are you really sure about this, going back to that memory place?"

"I have to," she told Kim. "There's nothing else I can do."

"But I could, you know, help you figure out some stuff, just the two of us."

"Not necessary. Next week everything's gonna be great." *No more sadness in the eyes,* she thought.

"Look. I'm really glad you confided in me. And I wasn't going to say this—but here goes. The way I see it, there's something you really should do first."

The elevator reached the fourteenth floor that wasn't really the fourteenth floor. Kim held her hand over the side of the door so it couldn't close.

"Talk to Evelyn," Kim said.

"No." The girl was adamant. She'd avoided nearly all contact with Evelyn for days. They'd barely seen each other. Meals were left on the stove so the girl could continue to eat in her room.

Evelyn, she had to admit, had respected her privacy admirably.

"Clara couldn't stand her," Kim said. "I don't think Rose got that close to her, either."

"Evelyn and Rose were perfectly friendly!" Though maybe, now that the girl thought about it, when Evelyn talked to her, Rose hadn't listened too carefully, changing the subject more often than not.

"Does Evelyn want this for you? How does she feel about it?"

The girl tightened her lips.

"Let me guess. You're not speaking to her."

The elevator started beeping. It didn't like to be held open too long.

"Why are you bringing this up?" the girl said. "You're supposed to be my cross-my-heart friend. It was very irresponsible of Evelyn, to let me do something irreversible."

"Oh, that's not fair. You were the one who wanted it. You still want it."

The beeping in the elevator got really loud.

"She gave her consent. She paid for it. She's the adult," the girl said.

"Right. That's why you should talk to her." Kim let go of the door. "Well, good luck finding that girl, whoever she is."

But I know exactly who she is, the girl thought, as the door closed. It was clear as day. *She's the girl I could've been, if life was fair.*

It was cool and gray at the bus stop. A few drops spattered her, but it never actually rained. The girl sensed she might not be coming back here anymore, which confused her, so she stayed a little longer.

I'll give the girl in the jean jacket one last chance.

As if it was the other way around, and the girl in the jean jacket was the one looking for *her.*

CHAPTER 30

She woke early Friday morning, long before dawn. Her lamp was on and cast a circle of light. It was quiet, middle-of-the-night quiet, with only a few cars on the expressway and hardly any planes.

She'd had another dream, unbearably vivid.

She was on a hydro-bus, heading home, standing room only. It was so crowded she couldn't even reach out for a pole to hold on to, and she tried to keep her balance as the bus lurched its way up and down the hills of Belle Heights. Next to her stood a man, tall as a tree. She looked at his face, saw those heavy-lidded eyes . . . she couldn't believe it. Her dad! Her dad was here! But he had died even before hydro-buses came to Belle Heights. So she didn't want to say anything, since that might break the spell or embarrass him because he was doing something impossible. Probably he would explain the misunderstanding of it to her later, how when everyone had thought he was dead, he'd just stayed out of sight for a while, but now he was here and here to stay. She was so happy—she was bursting with happiness.

Eventually she had to speak up. "Dad," she said casually, trying not to sound too excited, "it's our stop."

"You go on ahead. I have to be somewhere." His voice, still gentle, didn't have a smile in it, like it used to.

She didn't want to let him out of her sight. But she couldn't make a big deal out of it. It was important just to act normally, so then he could just show up later at home and everything would be the way it was supposed to be. She got off the bus— bad mistake. So stupid! Why hadn't she made up some excuse, that she had to be somewhere, too? She stared at the bus as it went down a hill. A woman was suddenly next to her, asking, "Did you leave something on the bus? I forgot my bag once. I called the office and they said it was in the Lost and Found."

Waking, the girl got a wrenching pain unlike anything she'd ever felt. A fist had tightened around her heart. She didn't blame Clara for climbing into a glass coffin and staying there. Who in her right mind would want to go through this? Strangely, though, she felt close to Clara here in this place, and it felt like a place, where Clara had never been.

She looked at Mr. Moore's painting, propped up on her bureau, and also out the window, at Belle Heights Tower, where Kim lived.

She got up and left the room.

Evelyn always slept with the door wide open and the curtains apart. In the almost-full moon, the girl could clearly see Evelyn's desk with her laptop, her tall mahogany bureau, and her bookshelf, where Clara had leafed through books by experts. Evelyn's bed was near the window, open just a crack. Her dark hair was spread across her pillow, and the gold necklace around her throat caught a glint of light. She was wearing a pale nightgown with a scoop neck that exposed one shoulder. A flowery kimono was draped over the foot of the bed.

The girl walked over to Evelyn, who smelled like lavender. She leaned down and gently nudged Evelyn's shoulder.

"Oh—" Evelyn stiffened and looked around urgently. "What— what time is it?"

"Late. Early."

Evelyn blinked to get used to the semidarkness. "Give me a minute. I'll get up."

"You don't have to." The girl hadn't realized she'd brought the bald elephant with her until she put it down on the bed. "I just want to say . . . I made you worry last week, when I stayed out so long. Before I went to Forget-Me-Not. I'm really sorry."

Evelyn seemed relieved—no emergency, apparently. "I didn't know what to think. If you were all right, if you were running away. . . . I tried to find you. I looked in the school directory and called your friends."

"You mean Kim and Cooper?"

"The ones you had lunch with. Selena Kearn and Astrid Mills."

But they weren't her friends. They weren't even each other's friends. The girl decided right then she would ask Mr. Slocum to switch her to different lab partners. Though he'd never done this before, she knew he would do it for her.

"I had to leave a message for Astrid, but Selena picked up," Evelyn said. "She told me you were with them at brunch and then you left. She also said something about a party here this Saturday—?"

The girl shook her head. "No, that's not happening." Astrid and Selena would definitely not be pleased that she was canceling it the day before it was supposed to happen. She could picture Selena, face burning behind her freckles, bitterly complaining she'd already promised everybody a DJ. She could even hear Astrid saying beneath her breath, "We were nice to you. You blew it."

"Evelyn," the girl said, "I should probably let you get back to sleep."

"That's okay. I'm awake." She sat up and leaned her back against the headboard.

"I always wondered." The girl hesitated. "I hope you don't mind my asking . . . why do you look in the mirror so much?"

Evelyn smiled a little. "My mother died quite young of skin cancer. I always have to look for moles, and keep at it, too. The cells in the body replace themselves so rapidly. Every seven years you have a whole new body."

Seven years—the amount of time Clara had spent in the glass coffin. "So I have a whole new body since Dad died."

"As do I." Evelyn nodded, taking this in. "It hasn't been so easy for us, has it?"

Evelyn had Sad Blue eyes, too.

"You tried telling me about your parents, once," the girl said. But Rose had had her mind on other things. "Could you tell me, again? I'm listening now."

"Well, my father was a drunk," Evelyn said matter-of-factly.

"And your mom?"

"Pretended he wasn't one. I grew up with . . . lies. They were everywhere, in every corner of every room. It was as if there was a terrible storm outside, and my parents kept looking out the window and declaring, 'It's a beautiful sunny day!' There were times I thought *I* was the crazy one. When my mother asked me a simple question—'How are you?'—I saw fear in her eyes. She didn't want the real answer. So I would say, 'Fine, just fine.' See why I never wanted to get married?"

"Except you did."

"It took me completely by surprise. Phil was always so honest. My father thought that promising something was the same thing as doing it. Phil kept his promises."

"But he didn't!" the girl said sharply. "He promised to keep me safe and sound."

"He kept that promise, too. You're here with me."

In fairy tales, the girl thought, the good parents died and the evil ones lived. But the fact that Evelyn had outlived her dad hadn't turned her into Evil Lynn. It just made her a single mom. The girl looked down, feeling something on her hand. Evelyn had taken hold of it for a few moments. It didn't feel like dead man's finger.

"I'm canceling it," the girl said.

"Yes, the party." Evelyn leaned back again.

"I don't mean that. I mean Forget-Me-Not."

Moonlight played on Evelyn's face. Her eyes widened.

There were only about thirty-five hours to go before this thing the girl had wanted so desperately.

"I'm shocked, too," the girl said.

"But I'm glad," Evelyn said.

CHAPTER 31

"Then," the girl began, "why didn't you stop me the first time?"

Evelyn reached over and picked up the bald elephant. "It made me . . . sick at heart. I worried that I was as bad as Phil, unable to say no to you. But it was the first thing you were ever willing to try. . . . I had to admire you for that." She put the elephant down. "I admire you still."

It came to the girl then, out of the blue.

Cora.

Clara had never given any thought to her name. Rose had picked a name that fit like a second skin, but maybe that meant a name you put on or slipped into, something added to the outside. This one seemed to come from deep inside. "Cora," she said, placing her hand on her chest. "My name."

Evelyn turned on her lamp and studied her carefully. "Cora it is."

Cora sat on the edge of the bed. "Dad used to sit on the side of my bed when he read to me."

"So patiently. He always read 'Snow-white' like it was completely new, even though the two of you already knew every word."

"That reminds me. There's this old movie based on 'Snow-white,' a screwball comedy. I might go see it Sunday—I have to talk to someone about that—but there's something else I'd like to do this weekend. With you, if that's okay."

"What's that?"

"Come on—I'll show you."

Evelyn got out of bed and took a moment to put her kimono on Cora's shoulders. Then they went to the desk, where Cora sat in the chair while Evelyn stood beside her. Cora tucked her hair behind both ears. She opened Evelyn's laptop and typed in "Australian cattle dog rescue."

"I only just heard about this kind of dog," Cora said. "I saw one, and then I saw another."

It turned out there were quite a few rescue centers up and down the East Coast, some not too far away, in New Jersey and Connecticut. Evelyn seemed interested. She went to the kitchen to grab a chair and bring it back with her. In the moonlight, they continued looking at the computer for some time, reading about the breed—highly intelligent, tenacious, needing lots of activity. And fiercely loyal, and protective of the people they live with.

Evelyn offered to borrow a company car to make the trip, and said, "We could make a day of it." Or several days, she added, to find the right dog.

Exactly, Cora thought. There was time.

ACKNOWLEDGMENTS

This book is dedicated to my awesome and insightful editor, Jordan Brown, with much gratitude and appreciation.

Many thanks to the excellent team at Balzer + Bray: Alessandra Balzer, Donna Bray, Renée Cafiero, Sarah Creech, Valerie Shea, Viana Siniscalchi, and Caroline Sun.

Special thanks to my wonderful agent, Susan Cohen at Writers House, and to others at Writers House, past and present, who were so generous with their help and suggestions: Trisha de Guzman, Brianne Johnson, Kelly Riley, and Kevin Webb.

Thanks to Jacob Hiss for a terrific book trailer, to Annie Farkas for lessons in stage makeup, to Dr. Ann Wayne Lucas and the staff at the Washington Square Animal Hospital, and to Dr. Gail Monaco for talking to me about grief in childhood.

Thanks to friends who heard me out: Marisha Chamberlain, Liz Rosenberg, Amy Tonsits, and Edra Ziesk.

Thanks to Tony Hiss, without whom . . . and for the best writing advice ever: "There's always a way."